Jenny will never forget her encounter with the stranger in the garden glade.

"Wait," he implored, and Jenny stopped, not looking at him. He wasn't touching her, but his voice held her captive. She didn't really want to go.

After what seemed an eternity, she shyly lifted her eyes to his. She thought his eyes would be laughing or mocking, but they were not. He seemed concerned.

"Why are you crying?" he asked, and she realized a tear had slipped down her cheek.

Because she was not adept in the art of lying, she simply told the truth. "I wanted to be near somebody. . .attractive. Just once in my lifetime. Something I could always remember."

His eyes held an element of surprise. "But you're engaged to be married," he said.

"I was forced into it," she said desperately. "I can't go through with it. I can't bear the thoughts of his. . ." She lowered her eyes and swallowed hard. "His kissing me or even touching me."

"I see," the gentleman said finally. He stepped closer. She felt his hand at the side of her waist. She lost her breath when he lifted her chin with his fingers, tilting her head back.

The silvery moon highlighted his handsome face. Time stood still while something deeper than moonlight burned in his dark eyes as they caressed her face. An eternity passed before his lips parted and she felt the warmth of his breath against her face. Instinctively, she leaned forward and closed her eyes. Her mouth trembled beneath his touch.

YVONNE LEHMAN, an award-winning novelist, lives in the heart of North Carolina's Smoky Mountains with her husband. They are the parents of four grown children. In addition to being an inspirational romance writer, she is also the founder of the Blue Ridge Christian Writers' Conference.

HEARTSONG PRESENTS

The Stranger's Kiss

Yvonne Lehman

Heartsong Presents

Yea, though I walk through the valley of the shadow of death,
I will fear no evil: for thou art with me;
thy rod and thy staff they comfort me.

PSALM 23:4

A note from the author:
*I love to hear from my readers! You may correspond with me
by writing:* **Yvonne Lehman**
Author Relations
PO Box 719
Uhrichsville, OH 44683

ISBN 1-58660-322-1

THE STRANGER'S KISS

All Scripture quotations, unless otherwise noted, are taken from
the King James Version of the Bible.

All of the characters and events in this book are fictitious. Any
resemblance to actual persons, living or dead, or to actual events
is purely coincidental.

Cover illustration by Nancy White Cassidy.

PRINTED IN THE U.S.A.

one

"Don't you know we would do our best to make a proper marriage for you after Emmie is married?" Aunt Christine snapped. "Must you take your own cousin's beaus?"

"What?" Jenny jumped up. "I would never do such a thing. How could I?" Although Jenny was three years older than Emmaline, she knew it only proper that Uncle Thomas and Aunt Christine's daughter be married before their poor relation. "I don't know what you're referring to," Jenny stammered, "or who you're talking about."

"Who?" Aunt Christine mimicked. "Don't pretend innocence with me, Jennifer. You know I mean Lord Bodley."

"What. . .what did he say?" she asked helplessly.

"What did he say?" Aunt Christine mimicked, glaring at Jenny with icy blue eyes full of venom. "Only that he wants to marry you!"

Dumbfounded, Jenny stumbled back, bruising her thigh against one arm of the chair as she sank into it. Now she understood why, from the moment she'd entered the drawing room, she'd felt like she must have unknowingly committed some dastardly deed.

Uncle Thomas stood with an arm propped on the mantle. The elegant clothes he wore gave him an air of distinction but could not hide the overweight of his middle years. His midsection protruded quite noticeably. His flushed face suggested that he and Aunt Christine had recently engaged in a heated discussion.

Aunt Christine's face had turned a deep scarlet. Her pale hair, adorned with jewels, was piled high on her head. Jenny felt her aunt overdressed for early morning, but she would have chosen her attire with Lord Bodley's visit in mind.

"I've never encouraged Lord Bodley," Jenny protested, gesturing helplessly. "I despise him. I'd rather die than marry Lord Bodley! Simply tell him that. He and Emmaline can marry. She is perfectly willing and would make Lord Bodley a fine wife."

"I'm afraid no amount of persuasion is going to change Bodley's mind. We certainly have tried." Aunt Christine lifted her hands and eyes toward the ceiling in exasperation.

Jenny stood and took a few steps toward them. "Surely Lord Bodley wants a wife equal to his social standing," she said. "I would not be acceptable in his circles."

"We exhausted every argument, Jenny," Uncle Thomas explained. "He has spoken to me about this matter on numerous occasions. It seems he is enamored not only by your looks, but also by what he calls your 'spirit' and quick tongue."

"I had hoped to put him off with that," Jenny wailed.

"Well, yes," Uncle Thomas said uncomfortably. "It has only served to entice and challenge Lord Bodley. And your background, Jenny, is as impressive as Lord Bodley's."

"Or it was," Aunt Christine interjected, "before your mother drove my brother to drink and ran off to America with that duke—"

"Christine," Uncle Thomas said in a warning tone.

Jenny gasped. "What?" Her heart began to pound. All her father had ever said while he was still living was that her mother had died and that they were never to speak of her.

Jenny touched her aunt's arm. "Did my mother die in America?"

"Never mind," Aunt Christine retorted. "It's enough to know that your mother disgraced the name of Greenough."

"Christine," Uncle Thomas implored.

Jenny's aunt sighed in exasperation.

"You see, Jenny," Uncle Thomas added calmly, "your situation of dire circumstances is not of your making. Lord Bodley understands that. He is willing to, um, look at Christine's family line, along with my own, which is not insignificant. He would not consider you an embarrassment. Any man would be fortunate. . ." His voice trailed off as he glanced toward his wife and found her glaring at him.

Jenny could not believe this. Uncle Thomas's every word, although apologetic—perhaps even complimentary—was clearing the way for her marriage with Lord Bodley to be not only acceptable but approved.

"How can I marry him?" Jenny argued. "I don't love him."

"Love?" her aunt spat. "Fiddlesticks."

Jenny glanced at Sir Thomas, who seemed busy studying the tips of his shiny black shoes. Did he wonder, as she did, if Aunt Christine had just implied that her own marriage was loveless?

Aunt Christine took a deep breath and continued in a barely controlled voice. "Few of us are so fortunate as to find love. A woman must think of her future, and it's a certainty," she said, rolling her eyes toward the ceiling again, "that you'll never get another chance like this one."

"I could never marry him," Jenny insisted. "Uncle Thomas, please. Can't you do something?"

The man shook his head. "Bodley will consider no one but you."

"But of course that's impossible," Jenny protested. "Surely you agree."

"We most certainly do not agree!" Aunt Christine answered forcefully. "You have taken your cousin's beau. The least you can do is have the decency to go through with it."

"You want me to marry him?" Jenny looked from her aunt to her uncle.

Aunt Christine lifted her head and a gleam came into her eyes. "Since Lord Bodley insists you are the only person who interests him, and he is willing to go to any lengths to get you," she answered with a sneer, "then yes, we do insist you marry him." After a pause, she continued. "He even resorted to blackmail."

"Blackmail?" Jenny queried.

"It seems your uncle Thomas lost fifty thousand pounds to Lord Bodley at the gaming tables. Now Bodley intends to collect."

Jenny walked over to face her uncle. "Uncle Thomas. You are selling me to repay a gambling debt?"

He shifted his weight from one foot to another, obviously discomfited. "It's not like that, Jenny," he replied. "He would have found another way. It's a good opportunity. One that may never come your way again."

"But I don't even like him," Jenny protested.

"Would you rather be committed to an asylum?" her aunt snapped.

"I'm old enough to go out on my own," Jenny countered. "I can start a school."

"According to the terms of the papers establishing our guardianship, we are your legal guardians until you're married," Aunt Christine reminded her. "If you defy us and refuse Lord Bodley, we can place you in an asylum."

Jenny shuddered. She'd heard of such terrifying places, but even that threat would not deter her. "Marrying Lord Bodley would be worse than an asylum," she declared, her head held high. "I will not do it."

Aunt Christine ignored her outburst. "You will do it, Jennifer," she said with an icy calm voice. "A guardian has complete and absolute power over his ward. It is our duty to see that you marry well. Besides, what parents would allow their children to attend a school where the mistress was a disobedient young wench? An unappreciative ingrate who defied her guardians?"

"But I'm not that," Jenny protested.

Her aunt's smug smile halted Jenny's words. "Exactly," the older woman agreed. "And being a sensible girl, you wouldn't allow such implications to be made about you."

Jenny knew this was no idle threat.

"Now," her aunt continued confidently, "Lord Bodley has asked for your hand in marriage. Your uncle and I have signed the settlements. Today I shall puff it off to the papers. Do you understand?"

Jenny felt trapped. Uncle Thomas remained silent. The awful thing was, she could see that from their point of view the situation was an opportunity of a lifetime. How could she ever have thought her personal desires would matter? Her own mother had abandoned her. Could she seriously expect more consideration from an aunt and uncle? She silently nodded her head in agreement.

"It seems Bodley has been planning this for some time," Aunt Christine explained, seeing the matter as settled. "The dressmakers will arrive this afternoon. Bodley says he will spare no expense. You will have whatever gowns you wish. All you have to do is snap your fingers."

"You mean," Jenny protested, "Lord Bodley is providing my very clothes?"

"Silence, Jennifer," Christine commanded. "You must learn to behave as a lady who will be escorted in royal circles, rather than as a schoolgirl who stands around with her tongue hanging out. Now," she directed, "next week we will go to Bodley House to announce the engagement."

"A week?" Jenny gasped. "I should have a year, at least. . . to prepare."

"Really, Jennifer, " her aunt chided. "You are twenty-one years old. And Bodley is a passionate man. He's very anxious for the marriage to take place. As I said, he is overcome with—"

"Oh, please," Jenny wailed, placing her hands over her ears

rather than hear about Lord Bodley's passions. His wicked words and grasping hands had already given evidence enough of such desires.

Turning quickly, she raced from the drawing room. Her steps did not slow until she came face-to-face with Emmaline, who stood poised at the bottom of the main staircase.

One look at her beet-red face and hostile eyes told Jenny that Emmaline had eavesdropped. "It is not my doing, Emmie," Jenny wailed helplessly, "and I won't go through with it."

Emmaline jerked away from Jenny's outstretched hand and ignored her imploring eyes. "That's prittle prattle and you know it," she snapped. Gathering up her pale lavender skirts, Emmaline turned with a flourish and stalked across the floor toward the drawing room.

Jenny could only race to her bedroom, but she refused to fall upon the coverlet, like one condemned to a fate mapped out for her by the likes of Ignatius, Lord Bodley.

Shivering, she looked out her windows. The pea soup fog that shrouded her view seemed to have crept inside her mind, for no clear escape from Bodley's preposterous proposal lay before her.

You're so like your mother, Aunt Christine had often said, as if that were something to be ashamed of. Suddenly Jenny's head lifted and she set her jaw. Perhaps that was her solution. Her mother had run away to America. Well, she could run away as well.

Determination fired her eyes. No matter what it took, she would escape marriage to Lord Bodley.

two

For days, Jenny lived with Emmaline's acute disappointment at losing Lord Bodley to her poor cousin. Emmaline stomped instead of walked, snapped rather than talked, and threw objects all over her bedroom. She slammed doors so hard that Jenny suspected they might fall from their hinges. Any protestations Jenny made about her unhappiness with the engagement fell on decidedly deaf ears.

One morning a seamstress arrived to measure Jenny for gowns and have her select materials. As she stood near the end of her bed, surrounded by the chattering woman and her imperious aunt, Jenny noticed her cousin pause at the open doorway.

"Don't stand out there gawking, Emmaline," Aunt Christine chided. "The seamstress will measure you for new gowns too."

"To soothe my ruffled feathers?" Emmaline snapped. She turned in a huff and headed toward her own bedroom.

At the end of the week, Emmaline's anger was further fueled by the arrival of an entourage of Bodley's servants to be at Jenny's disposal. They numbered more than the entire Cottingham household servants put together.

"The house is so overrun with servants, there's scarcely room enough to breathe," Aunt Christine complained whenever her daughter was within earshot, but Jenny observed that as soon as Emmaline left, Aunt Christine's face colored with excitement. The woman obviously relished giving orders right and left.

Perhaps it was because his gambling debt was cancelled by Bodley that Uncle Thomas strode around so importantly. He tried to suppress his pleasure when near Emmaline, but the look of satisfaction on his face was unmistakable. Jenny thought he smiled at her approvingly when the others weren't looking.

"I'll end up on the shelf," Emmaline wailed, one night at dinner. "My only prospect will be some dried-up old man with half a fortune."

"Don't be such a ninny," her mother chided. "As soon as this matter is settled, we can concentrate upon finding you a suitable husband."

Emmaline pushed her chair back from the table and stood up. "It was my understanding that's what we were doing all along," she countered viciously. "It was all a trick, wasn't it, Jenny? You were very clever when you pretended you hadn't set your cap for Bodley. You must have pinched your cheeks and bit your lips to make them rosy."

She threw her napkin onto her plate of half-eaten food and stalked away before Jenny could reply.

Although accustomed to Emmaline's tantrums and moods, Jenny regretted that she could not tell the sullen girl what was in her heart. She and Emmie had shared many good times when they had lived at their country home and ridden horses together across the meadows. They'd dreamed of their future. But after they moved to the London town house, Jenny began to feel the difference in their social standing.

Now with Bodley's proposal, everything had turned upside down. Instead of being a companion to Emmaline, Jenny had become the center of attention. She looked over at her aunt, who shook her head while chewing a bite of food. She knew Aunt Christine and Uncle Thomas would prefer this frantic activity to be centered on their daughter.

Aunt Christine took a sip of water. "At least," she said, stabbing another bite of food with her fork, "Bodley's money will be in the family."

૨ઠ

When the day of the engagement party arrived, Emmaline's

anger had receded into a sullen, stony silence. Jenny knew she could say nothing to redeem herself in her cousin's eyes. In all honesty, Jenny couldn't say she didn't enjoy the change of routine and status. It was almost a fairy tale existence—except for Bodley, whose likeness fell far short of the handsome prince in such fantasies. Jenny could visualize his swarthy face. She'd seen his jiggling movement, especially when he swung his cane forward when he walked. When she'd accompanied him and Emmaline on an outing, she'd watched the movement of his arms, revealing the fur lining of his cape. A top hat had covered the almost naked crown of his head, while wisps of thin brownish hair curled above his ears and at the back of his snowy white neckcloth.

He cannot buy me. But it was necessary that Aunt Christine, Uncle Thomas, and Lord Bodley believe she had accepted the proposed marriage as her destiny.

Aunt Christine's words, about Jenny's mother running away to America, kept racing through Jenny's mind. The more she thought of the idea, the more it intrigued her. But any means of escape would be useless unless she had convinced everyone that she had agreed to this outrageous charade. Until such a time, her aunt and uncle would certainly continue their everwatchful attendance.

"You look lovely, M'Lady," said one of the attendants, bringing Jenny's thoughts back to the task at hand.

"Thank you, Mindy," Jenny murmured, staring at her reflection. She wore cheek rouge and powder. Her dark hair was arranged fashionably with several dark curls gracing her fair, clear complexion and the back of her long, graceful neck. Yet another curl fell along the front of one shoulder, where the lace of the dress ended and the satin began. The rest of her raven hair was piled high on her head. For the first time, her lips were painted a rosy red.

Jenny had decided that this one evening she would dress as

she liked. After the event was over, she must drop out of sight, perhaps even change her name, in order to start a life of her own. She was not concerned with public approval, for those above the class of governess, companion, or tutor had never recognized her in social circles, nor had Emmaline required her friends to include Jenny as an equal.

❧

The time came to go to Bodley House. Jenny had not allowed the Cottinghams to see her dress during its making. Now, Uncle Thomas, Aunt Christine, and Emmaline stood at the foot of the stairs as Jenny descended. She rather hoped her aunt and uncle would consider her choice of color scandalous and not allow the engagement party to take place.

Jenny's deep burgundy gown was cut fashionably low in front. Unaccustomed to exposing her skin, as did the parading debutantes, Jenny had insisted upon an inlay of sheer burgundy lace, in a rose pattern, to form a high scalloped neckline. Three gathered ruffles fell gracefully over her shoulders, forming the illusion of puffed and gathered sleeves. The hemline draped into folds, exposing light rose-colored ruffles, the peaks adorned with burgundy satin roses.

The ruffles matched the color of her evening gloves. Bodley, having discovered the color of her dress from a servant, had sent jewels for her to wear. Clusters of roses, set with diamonds and rubies, graced her earlobes and left wrist.

Looking distinguished in his evening clothes and graying hair, Uncle Thomas stared at Jenny. His face paled. Without a word he turned and headed for the front door.

Emmaline, wearing a dazed expression, forgot she was not speaking to Jenny except to ridicule or snap. "You look different," she said.

Jenny could have replied that she hadn't chosen to grow up overnight. She preferred to be that young girl who had ridden through the park with Emmaline not long ago and giggled about the eligible young men.

"It's a lovely dress," Aunt Christine admitted stiffly. "But you might have picked something less flamboyant for an engagement party. Something white." She sighed with resignation. "On second thought," she murmured, "that's exactly what Bodley would want. His tastes have apparently been tainted by the world."

Jenny inwardly winced at the insult, but she had already determined that, degrading as it was to have to go to such a party and pretend she liked the idea of being bought by Ignatius, Lord Bodley, she would bide her time. Soon, she would bear no more insults.

Jenny knew she looked more fetching than ever in her life. She had always detested the pale colors that Emmaline wore which complimented her cousin's fair skin, light hair, and gray eyes. Emmaline looked attractive in them, but they did nothing for Jenny's dark coloring and deep blue eyes.

"You look lovely, Emmie," Jenny complimented, admiring her cousin's pale yellow gown with white lace ruffles. The younger girl would have no trouble attracting young men, now that they knew Lord Bodley's attentions were directed elsewhere.

"Thank you," Emmaline said stiffly and then hurried toward the door. Aunt Christine, dressed in blue satin, followed her daughter.

Lord Bodley had sent his own carriage pulled by four black horses to convey Jenny to his house that evening.

"You girls ride in Bodley's carriage," directed Uncle Thomas. "Lady Cottingham and I will take ours."

Emmaline hesitated, then grudgingly obeyed. Jenny tried to make conversation, but Emmaline pretended not to hear and looked into the darkness outside the windows of the carriage.

"I'm not going through with this, Emmie," Jenny said doggedly. She watched as Emmaline's reserve wavered. Finally her cousin looked at her.

"You know there's no way out, Jenny. Once my mother has made up her mind about something, there's no changing it."

"But there has to be a way." Jenny leaned forward. "Help me, Emmie," she pleaded.

"What can I do, Jenny?" Emmaline asked miserably. "Bodley wants you. And from the fuss he's made, nothing will change his mind."

Jenny's eyes flashed as she spoke excitedly. "We'll have you marry him. You can wear a heavy veil so he won't know. Then he can later be surprised that it was you instead of me."

Emmaline broke out in the first genuine laugh Jenny had heard from her in days. "Oh, Jenny. Your fantasies again. It would be funny if it were not so serious. Bodley deserves to have something like that done to him." Her voice dropped. "Only if it were someone else instead of me."

"Maybe if you told him of your love, Emmaline."

Emmaline stared at her in wonder. "Love, Jenny? I have never loved Ignatius Bodley."

Jenny gasped. "But you said you wanted to marry him."

"I'm more realistic than you, Jenny, even if I am younger," Emmaline replied. "To have married Ignatius, with all his connections, was beyond even my wildest dreams. Now, to think he courted me just to get to you." She clenched her gloved hands. "It's humiliating, but I have to go tonight and pretend I don't care in front of all those people who suspect I do. Frankly I'd rather see Ignatius, Lord Bodley in his grave!"

"Oh, Emmie," Jenny gasped. She quickly looked away from Emmaline's distraught face. Then she admitted quietly, "I too would rather see Lord Bodley in his grave, than in my marriage bed."

Through the carriage window, she glimpsed the lamps illuminating the front of Lord Bodley's London home. Unless her plans were successful, that home would soon become her prison.

three

The Cottinghams and Jenny joined other guests alighting from their carriages and stepping down onto red carpet which stretched from the sidewalk to the main steps in honor of the occasion. The soft glow of candlelight illuminated every window in the impressive mansion, one of Bodley's many residences scattered across England.

When shown to her private suite on the second floor, Jenny thought of the many times she had been separated from the Cottinghams at fine houses. Whereas then she had been placed with other companions, now Bodley had elevated her position. She wished she might discover that she was wrong about his character and find he had some redeeming qualities she could learn to love.

But as she descended the main stairs, feeling all eyes upon her, a sudden wave of distaste swept over her. She recalled the party at Lady Cramerson's two weeks earlier. During one of Jenny's unguarded moments, Bodley had maneuvered her to a spot behind a potted palm.

Such shenanigans had been a game of his since she had first made an appearance when the season had begun. He had played not only hide-and-seek, but also touch-and-grin. Such behavior was often tolerated by servants, whose livelihood depended upon their jobs, but she was in no such position.

"I'm Emmaline's companion," she'd reminded him staunchly. "Not in your class, my lord." It had taken every ounce of her self-control not to tell him what she really thought about his ungentlemanly behavior.

"If Lady Emmaline were to become my wife, would you

accompany her to my household as companion or milady's personal maid?" he'd asked, a sly grin upon his face.

"I would not," she retorted, forgetting for a moment that Aunt Christine had warned her not to do anything that might harm Emmaline's chances with Lord Bodley. Her dark eyes flashed fire. "Already I have assisted in the schoolroom," she informed him. "I will become a teacher. Or," she added, inching away from him, "I might even take a job in a factory."

He threw back his head and laughed. "Ah, my little spitfire. You do not belong in a factory." He leered and thrust forth a sweaty hand.

Gasping, Jenny swatted at his hand. "I'll scream," she warned.

"And I'll say you saw a mouse," he answered with a triumphant smile.

Now, as Jenny descended the stairs, she felt like a mouse caught in Lord Bodley's trap. There was nowhere to hide. Forcing a neutral expression onto her face, she extended her hand to Bodley's outstretched one. He bent down and planted a slobbery kiss upon the back of it. Jenny forced her lips to curve in a slight smile.

Leading her to the entrance of the great ballroom, Bodley himself, with Uncle Thomas and Aunt Christine in close pursuit, introduced her to his guests. The experience simply reinforced her opinions of those who looked down their aristocratic noses at the lower social classes.

"Oh, I had no idea that Emmaline had such a delightful cousin," one grand lady exclaimed, although she had often visited the Cottinghams' London home.

"I did not know Sir Thomas and Lady Cottingham were blessed with such a lovely niece," other guests murmured.

Jenny knew they had seen her at other events when she had served as Emmaline's companion. Or perhaps they had not seen her, but had taken her for granted as a necessary convenience, like a piece of furniture.

Jenny could not dwell long upon the hypocrisy of so many of the guests, for she was obligated to dance with her intended. She attempted conversation, but he only praised her beauty and complimented her on her choice of gown. He held her much too tightly, despite her protests. Any faint hope of a decent life with Bodley became more unlikely with each passing moment.

Jenny had been dancing for almost an hour when she noticed the man. He stood at the top of the staircase, leaning against the banister. She thought him quite handsome and wondered if he were evaluating the young ladies from that vantage point, wondering if any present might make him a suitable wife. Then she blushed at the thought, for his eyes seemed to follow her wherever she went.

Despite all attempts not to do so, Jenny found herself looking for the man who changed positions every so often. She wondered if he would ask her to dance, but he did not. When other men danced with her, she pretended they were the stranger—so incredibly handsome, tall, elegant, and mysterious.

Smiling, she allowed herself to glide over the dance floor, except when Bodley held her so tightly she could scarcely breathe. She avoided his leering gaze but could not escape the uncomfortable feel of his hot, raspy breath on her neck. He was not much taller than herself, she realized. And he was overweight. His ruddy face did not help matters, nor his lewd remarks about what they would do once they were married.

She began to realize the advantages of being plain and wished she had not dressed up so much. But, she told herself, it wouldn't have mattered. He had made his advances even when she'd worn youthful garments and her hair had been braided in a style appropriate for a prim young companion.

❧

The stranger knew he must remain as inconspicuous as possible, without raising suspicion that he was deliberately doing so. And it was not difficult to remain at the top of the staircase under the circumstances.

His eyes could not get their fill of her. They gazed upon Jenny, followed her every step, assessed her every move. He had become mesmerized—spellbound by her beauty, her grace, and what appeared to be playful attempts at assuaging her ardent admirer, soon to become her husband. She was Bodley's intended! That thought wrenched his heart. How could she be attracted to such a bloke as Bodley? But of course, he knew. Bodley had been the highest bidder for her hand, what else?

But now that I've found her, how can I let her go? That was impossible. Now that he had found her, saw her, he must meet her, speak with her. With the dark thoughts that penetrated his mind, a shadow passed over his countenance, as he contemplated in his heart and mind what he must do.

❧

Jenny did not see the stranger during the seven course dinner. Sir Thomas's formal announcement of the engagement at the end of the meal received applause. After the requisite toasts, the ladies rose to leave the men in private for their customary drinks and conversations. As Jenny started toward the door, the handsome stranger passed by her. He paused briefly, only long enough to make eye contact, and she saw that his eyes were a dark brown, almost black. His eyes gleamed as he looked on her with apparent approval. He seemed different from the other men she had met at Bodley's party, but although she intended to look at him boldly and flash him a charming smile, she instead found herself suddenly quite shy.

Jenny reprimanded herself for the blush she felt on her cheeks. She lowered her eyelids and felt a quickening of her breath. When she looked up again, he nodded politely, then turned away and moved swiftly toward Bodley's table.

While throughout the evening all of the ladies had indicated a willingness to accept Jenny's new-found position, they did not push their attentions upon her as the ladies broke into smaller groups and strolled the huge formal gardens. For the most part, they left her alone. She had been the poor relation of Emmaline's, and although she knew of no enemies among the aristocracy, neither had she formed any close friendships with this privileged group.

Jenny walked through the gardens, along a narrow path for some distance, then came to a small glade in the midst of trees and fragrant blooming shrubs. Beneath a tree sat a small table and two chairs. A warm breeze stirred the tender green leaves, gently lifting them. The full moon's silvery sheen filtered down between the branches, creating an ethereal setting.

Surrounded by such enchantment, Jenny did not want to think of her predicament or of her future. For the moment she preferred to escape with her fantasies. Lifting her face to gaze through an opening in the canopy of tree limbs, she glimpsed the shimmering stars. If one wished hard enough, surely dreams would come true.

❧

In the dining room, the gentlemen raised their voices to a loud and boisterous pitch. They made comments and joked in a way that could not be done in the presence of ladies. Bodley himself poured drinks for everyone. Then Sir Thomas, reveling in his position as guardian of the bride-to-be, took a pinch of snuff from his silver box, as was the mark of a fashionable gentleman, and offered to pour the next round of drinks. He graciously handed Bodley his drink, then proceeded around the table, toasting the forthcoming marriage. After these were downed, another gentleman offered yet another toast.

The stranger inched his way back until he reached the doorway, slipped from the room, and hastily exited. Outside, he looked around but could not find the one he sought. Thinking himself unobserved, he slipped around to the darkest part of the garden, found a path, and followed it into the more heavily wooded area.

ஐ

Hearing footfalls, Jenny's heart began to pound, fearing it might be Bodley. Bringing her hand to her throat, she gasped as a gentleman stepped into the glade. He stood still a moment, not taking his eyes from her, then set his drink on the small table. He coughed lightly and seemed about to speak.

Jenny felt a sudden instinct to lower her eyes and run because of the quivery feeling his presence evoked. But no, she told herself, she would not be shy. She might be forced to spend the rest of her life with the grasping arms and the slobbering mouth of Lord Bodley. This might be the only chance she'd ever have for a moment like this. If forced into the arms of Bodley, she would dream of this encounter. She wanted to be like a heroine in a novel and rush into the stranger's arms. With one quick step she moved toward him, but just as they were close enough to touch, she turned away quickly and stumbled. Reaching out her hand she caught hold of the table.

Embarrassed by her forward actions, Jenny felt her face growing warm. She had made a goose of herself. She was about to turn and run when his voice stopped her.

"Wait," he implored, and she stopped, not looking at him. He wasn't touching her, but his voice held her captive. She didn't really want to go.

After what seemed an eternity, she shyly lifted her eyes to his. She thought his eyes would be laughing or mocking, but they were not. He seemed concerned.

"Why are you crying?" he asked, and she realized a tear had slipped down her cheek.

Because she was not adept in the art of lying, she simply told the truth. "I wanted to be near somebody. . .attractive. Just once in my lifetime. Something I could always remember."

His eyes held an element of surprise. "But you're engaged to be married," he said.

"I was forced into it," she said desperately. "I can't go through with it. I can't bear the thoughts of his. . ." She lowered her eyes and swallowed hard. "His kissing me or even touching me."

"I see," the gentleman said finally. He stepped closer. She felt his hand at the side of her waist. She lost her breath when he lifted her chin with his fingers, tilting her head back.

The silvery moon highlighted his handsome face. Time stood still while something deeper than moonlight burned in his dark eyes as they caressed her face. An eternity passed before his lips parted and she felt the warmth of his breath against her face. Instinctively, she leaned forward and closed her eyes. Her mouth trembled beneath his touch, as his lips moved, caressed, and gently explored her lips.

Jenny felt limp, despite his supporting arm. Then, surprised at her own boldness, she lifted her arms and wrapped them around his neck. He did not protest, but pulled her tightly against himself. His lips took control of hers in a demanding, lingering kiss.

Suddenly, he stopped. A low moan escaped his throat and he held her head against his chest. His fingers caressed a curl, and their touch thrilled the skin at the nape of her neck. She wondered if it were her heart, or his, that was thundering so. Her whole being felt alive as never before. She felt safe and protected and wished she never had to move.

"My!" he said finally, shakily. "I feel rather faint."

Jenny turned her head to look up into his handsome face. A strange expression hovered about his dark eyes.

"I think," Jenny said low and breathlessly, "in the novels, it is the lady who feels faint."

He chuckled and moved back, holding her away by the shoulders. "That was your first kiss?" he asked with incredulity.

"Well, Lord Bodley has moved his slobbery lips past mine, but I never let them stay," she affirmed. She hesitated and spoke low. "Now I am glad."

"Was it all you expected?" he asked seriously.

Jenny closed her eyes and hugged her arms to herself. "Oh, so much more. I shall always remember it. No matter what. I have something to dream of for the rest of my life." She suddenly looked at him with tenderness. "Thank you," she said. "Thank you so very much."

The stranger took a deep breath, then smiled. "My pleasure, I assure you, my lady." He reached for her hand, turned it over, and gently placed his lips on its palm.

"I would do anything to get out of this coil I'm in," she said suddenly, as he let go of her hand.

"Anything?" he questioned, raising his expressive eyebrows.

Jenny was not quite sure she knew what she meant by that statement. After a few moments, she nodded. "Yes, I think so."

He started to say something when they heard someone calling, "Jenny! Where is my sweet Jenny?"

Jenny stiffened. Fear filled her heart.

A look of distress crossed the gentleman's face. "I must go," he said hastily. "Don't worry. I will come for you tomorrow. But do not mention having seen me or anything about me. All right?"

Jenny didn't understand, nevertheless, she nodded. The stranger disappeared into the woods, just as Lord Bodley entered the glade. She looked around for the stranger, but he was gone. She wondered if she had imagined the whole thing. She had read that people did that sometimes when situations were unbearable. But she could not have imagined the tingling sensation his kiss had awakened on her lips and throughout her being. She detested the thought of Bodley intruding upon that emotion.

"Ah, there you are, my pretty," Bodley said, holding a

glass. He took a big swallow and set the goblet on the table. "I thought you would be waiting here for me."

Bodley reached for her, and she barely managed to dodge his hands. He smelled heavily of strong drink. With a strength unknown to her, she pushed Bodley away. He swayed back a little, laughed, picked up a goblet from the table, and drank from it.

Jenny asked quickly, "Do you know I have no dowry?"

He shook his head. "Don't care," he said. "I have enough for both of us. You'll never want for anything. I knew you were beautiful, but tonight is more than I egs. . .espec. . .ecs. . ."

He shook his head as if trying to clear it, laughed, and emptied the contents of the goblet down his throat. Then he awkwardly set the goblet down and drank from the other one.

He started toward her. Jenny put out her hand.

"Did you know," she asked firmly and loudly, hoping to penetrate his mind if it was still functioning, "that my mother was an immoral woman?"

His eyes opened wide momentarily. "No," he droned, rather taken aback.

"Yes," Jenny said with renewed bravery. "She caused a terrible scandal, and when it is known you will be a laughingstock."

"Ah, ha!" he said and a lecherous expression crossed his face. He raked her body with his eyes. "I knew there was something different about you," he slurred. "A doxy, eh? I like that, by George. I really like that."

Jenny realized her confession had only served to incite him further. He staggered nearer.

"I don't love you, Lord Bodley," she said firmly.

"You'll learn, my sweet," he said with confidence and again drank from the goblet.

Jenny felt helpless. She couldn't bear to be alone with such a disgusting man for even a few minutes. How could she spend a lifetime with him? She moaned, lifted her skirt, managed a sidestep away from the drunken man, and ran from the glade, uncomfortably aware that while she had temporarily made her escape, she had also succeeded in becoming more of a challenge to him.

❧

Lady Christine and Emmaline were standing by a fountain in the garden near the back of Bodley House when suddenly Jenny ran up to them from the path. She looked at Emmaline. "He won't listen to reason," she wailed. "But somehow I will get out of this. I promise, Emmaline, if it's the last thing I do."

Several women standing nearby turned their heads and stared at the distraught young woman as she ran into the house.

Speaking in a whisper so that others would not hear her, Lady Christine said to her daughter, "That girl's going to get a thrashing if she upsets these plans. Go talk to him, Emmaline. Soothe his ruffled feathers."

Seeing the hesitation in Emmaline's eyes, Lady Christine murmured, "Even if they go through with this marriage, she will end up like her mother, and he will be on the market again. It wouldn't hurt, my dear, for you to be gracious and compliant. When his ardor has abated, then he will see you for the lady that you are."

Emmaline still didn't look pleased with the situation, but she nonetheless made her way to the glade. Almost immediately she returned. "He just sits there drinking and mumbling, shaking his head," she reported to her mother. "Jenny must have really upset him. He didn't even realize I spoke to him."

"Perhaps we can get him to come back inside. I'll see what I can do." Lady Christine headed for the glade. A few minutes later she returned. "Lord Bodley has fallen to the ground," she announced with alarm. "He's thrashing about. Oh, I'm afraid he's quite ill."

She rushed to the back door. "Please help," she said to a

gentleman inside. "Lord Bodley needs assistance."

Several gentlemen followed Lady Christine to the glade.

৵

Inside the house, Jenny descended the main stairs, carrying her wrap and evening bag. Upon rushing in a few minutes earlier, she had pled with her uncle to take her home. He had, to her surprise, agreed to do so immediately.

Now, she and Sir Thomas stared as men carried in the trembling Bodley, mumbling incoherently. His eyes rolled back into his head.

"Too much to drink," said one gentleman uneasily, while another laughed nervously.

"Our apologies, ladies," said another.

"Get him to his bedroom," suggested a perturbed guest.

With extreme effort, several men managed to hoist the uncooperative Bodley up the stairs.

"We should indeed leave," Sir Thomas said, as if mortified at Bodley's condition. Other guests expressed similar sentiments.

Just then Sir James Crittenbough came down the stairs, his face pale. "I say, Sir Thomas," he said, "could you ensure that a doctor is summoned?"

"A doctor?" Sir Thomas questioned.

"Indeed," Sir Crittenbough replied, glancing toward the ladies as if concerned that he would alarm them. "I suspect Sir Bodley needs a doctor immediately."

"Very well," Sir Thomas replied. "I will fetch him myself."

Crittenbough turned to the ladies. "You will perhaps be more comfortable in the drawing room," he said unevenly.

"What is it?" Lady Christine ventured to ask.

"Too much drink, I'm sure," Crittenbough replied, but his voice revealed the concern he attempted to conceal.

The merriment of the occasion had already died away, and silent gentlemen stood back from the elegant staircase. Other gentlemen lined the elaborate hallway above. The ladies gathered in the drawing room where they exchanged a few words in quiet tones.

Finally, the doctor arrived and hurried up the stairs, followed by Sir Thomas.

Soon Sir Thomas descended the stairs and came into the drawing room. Several other men followed and walked over to their ladies.

"Lord Bodley has. . .expired," Sir Thomas said, his last word barely audible.

Lady Christine put her hand to her throat and drew herself up. Emmaline let out a startled scream, then stifled it with her hand. The first thought that entered Jenny's mind was that she would not have to marry Bodley, but the situation seemed so unreal that she felt numb, experiencing neither joy nor regret. Looking up to find her uncle staring at her, Jenny wondered if he expected her to collapse.

"Let us leave, Thomas," Lady Christine said, picking up her skirts to move forward.

"I'm afraid, my dear," he said pointedly, "such action is not recommended."

The women stared at him questioningly.

"You see," he explained, "the doctor is asking guests kindly not leave the premises. He has summoned the magistrate."

·&·

The magistrate, after consulting with the doctor and learning about both Bodley's convulsions and his loss of control of bodily functions, agreed that the symptoms were more extreme than would usually be expected from drunkenness. However, he announced that he would leave the determination of cause of death to the coroner. In the meantime, he asked the exquisitely attired guests to volunteer any information that might shed light on the regrettable situation. Everyone agreed that Bodley had an incredible tolerance for drink and had actually imbibed less than usual that evening, because he had been preoccupied much of the time with his lovely intended.

The magistrate's suspicions increased by the moment, however, when he heard the remarks of the three ladies who, one at a time, had been alone with Lord Bodley in the glade. According to them and the doctor Lord Bodley had progressed from seeming drunkenness, to incoherence, stupor, convulsions, coma, and then ultimately to death.

Immediately, the magistrate determined he would visit the glade. "Bring me lanterns," he commanded the servants, who hurried to obey. When the magistrate reached the glade, he muttered, "Now, that's odd." Lifting the goblet toward the brilliant moonlight, he saw dregs of something in the bottom of the glass. "Well, well," he added as he observed a faint ring of fine white dust near the rim of the glass.

The magistrate allowed the guests to return to their homes, but he sternly advised them to stay in London. He took the goblet with him, along with a guest list he obtained from the butler. Clearly, this was not the end of the matter.

Later that night, the coroner determined what the doctor and the magistrate had suspected. Lord Bodley had been the victim of arsenic poisoning. The victim's excessive drinking had hastened the effects of the poison.

Arsenic could be found in the pantry of any household, even the magistrate's, because it was used to kill rats. The most amateur killer would have easy access to the poison. The magistrate shrugged in resignation. The next day he would begin the difficult task of questioning members of the aristocracy with due sensitivity.

❧

The next morning, Jenny ate breakfast in her room. The Cottinghams had been pointedly silent on the ride home the night before, she assumed because their dreams of further social prestige had died with Bodley.

At midmorning, the magistrate arrived, and a servant soon notified Jenny that she was wanted for questioning in the parlor. She entered the room, and the magistrate motioned for her to shut the door. Jenny complied and quietly took a seat.

"Did Lord Bodley's drinking habits repel you?" the magistrate asked.

"Yes," Jenny replied, determined to answer truthfully.

"And you were unhappy about your engagement to Lord Bodley," he quietly stated.

Jenny wondered where he had learned that fact. "I did not love him," she replied softly, reluctant to speak ill of the deceased.

"Now about last evening," the magistrate continued, "when Lord Bodley met with his untimely death."

After reviewing the information she had given him the night before, the magistrate dismissed Jenny—for the moment. Soon he asked her down again to answer questions about her situation with the Cottinghams. Jenny readily praised her relatives for their kind and generous care for her during the past eight years. Once again she was dismissed.

But that afternoon, she was called into the parlor for a third time. Immediately, she recognized that the magistrate's tone had changed. For several long moments, he simply looked at her.

Then he asked sternly, "Are you positive that you have nothing, nothing more to relate?"

She could think of nothing more.

"Very well," he said, and took his leave.

"Perhaps that's the end of the matter," Aunt Christine said, as soon as the front door closed behind the magistrate. "Surely he's aware we've told all we know."

"It would seem so," Uncle Thomas replied. "Please— enough unpleasantness. Let us speak of other matters."

"I think he's going to accuse someone," Emmaline said, her

fair skin paler than usual. "Isn't that the purpose of the entire investigation?"

No one replied. Throughout the rest of the day and into dinner that evening, Jenny noticed that everyone seemed to be lost in their own thoughts. Even the servants performed their tasks with bland faces and downcast eyes.

Jenny picked at her food, feeling a strange queasiness in her stomach. The evening before at Bodley's house, she'd felt the magistrate had regarded her with respect as Bodley's intended. Yet today his words had held elements of accusation. Much as she tried to shrug off her concerns, Jenny knew in her heart that something was decidedly wrong.

▲

The following day, the magistrate, accompanied by two Bow Street runners, requested that the Cottinghams, including Jenny, accompany him to a London courtroom.

The four members of the family stood in front of the chief magistrate, who questioned them extensively but uncovered no new information. At last he asked the Cottinghams to wait in a small room while he consulted with the other magistrates.

"I don't like this," Uncle Thomas stated as soon as the door was shut. "I don't like this one bit. There is no reason for us to be called down here unless they suspect one of us committed the dastardly deed."

Jenny's stomach suddenly felt hollow. She thought she would be sick. She had done nothing wrong, but why did she have this sense of foreboding?

"They need to take some action quickly," Uncle Thomas continued, apparently unaware of Jenny's nervousness. "The public demands swift justice in such cases because such a poisoning could happen to anyone—the poison being so readily available."

After what seemed like hours, the Cottinghams were finally summoned back to the courtroom. Jenny was instructed to stand before the chief magistrate.

"The evidence weighs heavily," he announced gravely. "The motive is clear." His eyes bore into Jenny's. "Did you not make the statement many times that you would not go through with the marriage to Lord Bodley?"

"Yes, but. . ."

He held up his hand, halting her words. "The motive is clear," he continued. "The accessibility to the poison posed no problem. Only one goblet had any trace of arsenic in it, and it was discovered in the glade where Bodley had taken ill. Numerous eyewitnesses have given identical accounts of who had gone toward and who had run from the glade where Ignatius, Lord Bodley became ill and thereafter expired."

Jenny was stunned. Did these men seriously think she had poisoned Bodley?

"Apparently this is the work of an amateur, an emotional female who had not thought through her actions," the chief magistrate asserted. "Yet, the deed itself must be judged premeditated. The engaged couple spent considerable time in the glade. Only two others had gone to the glade after Jennifer had run into the garden, quite distraught, affirming her intentions of not going through with the marriage. Her statements had been overheard by several witnesses.

"I and my colleagues have questioned you several times," he added pointedly, his voice becoming stronger by the moment. "We felt you held something back and hoped our suspicions would prove to be unfounded. However, the evidence is overwhelming."

The chief magistrate took a deep breath and announced in a dispassionate voice, "Miss Jennifer Cottingham, regretfully we have no alternative but to accuse you of the premeditated murder of Ignatius, Lord Bodley." Jenny had never fainted in her life, but upon hearing those words, darkness enveloped her, blocking out all reality.

four

When Jenny regained consciousness, the first thing she saw was the incredulous, horrified faces of the Cottinghams.

"You will immediately be placed in custody. Please follow the matron," the chief magistrate ordered. A large-boned, middle-aged woman helped Jenny to her feet and began to escort her out of the courtroom by a side door. As Jenny looked back at the Cottinghams, who seemed stunned into silence, she felt as if she had already been condemned. Her last sight before walking through the door and into a waiting coach was of Emmaline burying her face in a lace-edged handkerchief.

At least she was taken to a house, rather than to Newgate Prison, Jenny consoled herself. Her room was on the third floor, with walls covered in peeling gray paint, a bed for herself, a cot for the matron, a straight chair in front of a small dresser, a rocking chair, and a chest. When Jenny approached the small open window, the matron, who had introduced herself as Mrs. Millet, hurried to close it a tad, and Jenny knew the woman feared her prisoner might jump through it in an attempt to escape.

None of Jenny's personal items had been brought to her, and she still wore her plain gray dress. Attempted conversation failed completely. Jenny did not like the silent speculation of the matron, who seemed wary and watchful, lest Jenny attempt some dastardly deed.

"May I have something to read?" Jenny asked.

"We shall see," the matron replied, then asked the woman who brought the supper tray to look into the matter. Over an hour later the woman tapped on the door and mentioned the vicar. After closing the door, the matron handed Jenny a Bible.

Jenny lay on the bed, propped up against a pillow, and tried to read. She had read some Scripture before and, wanting to rid herself of fearful thoughts about her uncertain future, she turned to the love story of Ruth and Boaz. She loved the story of the poor young woman who had won the favor of a wealthy, kind man. She'd often dreamed that such a fate would befall her, but she wasn't sure about that anymore. She had met such a man, yet he had instructed her not to mention his presence and disappeared into the night. Then Bodley had died, and she now stood accused of murder.

She shuddered, unable to concentrate on the pages. She believed in God, of course, and had prayed to Him in the past—when she needed her mother and wanted her father to stop drinking. But God hadn't answered those prayers. If He cared about her, would He have allowed this to happen? She thought not. She closed the book. Never had she felt so frightened or alone.

❧

The following morning, Jenny's fears increased. "You think I killed him," Jenny accused her aunt Christine, who had brought some of her personal items. "How could you think that about me?"

"Oh, Jenny. We don't know what to think," her aunt said uncomfortably, sitting on the edge of the bed near Jenny and twisting her handkerchief. "I should have realized how desperate you were. We really thought it best. I should have recalled. . ."

Aunt Christine stopped as if it were useless to continue, and Jenny knew she was about to refer to her mother. Her mother had been desperate enough to abandon her husband and child. Did Aunt Christine really believe Jenny had been desperate enough to commit murder?

"What will happen to me?" Jenny whispered.

Aunt Christine hesitated before saying, "We've only been told that you will soon be removed."

"Removed?" Jenny questioned, bewildered. She did not like the sound of that.

Aunt Christine nodded, and Jenny asked what that meant.

"I don't really know," Christine replied. "Your uncle Thomas has been asked to relinquish his guardianship, and someone, I don't know who, will provide you with legal assistance."

"How can that be?" Jenny cried. These were her relatives. Her only flesh-and-blood relatives. "To. . .a stranger? Who? Why? What does it mean?"

Aunt Christine stood and paced the floor, fanning her face as if the surroundings suffocated her. Finally she turned toward Jenny.

"No doubt someone who read of your plight in the newspapers took pity on you. An unidentified person sent a representative to Sir Thomas and paid him a considerable sum to do this. Your uncle admits this is highly irregular, however it has been done legally and with the approval of the authorities. Already, you have gained the sympathy of the courts, and this person, whoever he may be, is apparently much better able to help you than our family. It is for your own good."

For her own good? It had been for her own good that she had been promised to Bodley. Now, Uncle Thomas had relinquished his responsibility to someone else, at a time when she needed help so desperately.

"But I'll never see you again. I'll be taken to prison. Oh, Aunt Christine." Jenny reached out her arms. Christine sat down on the edge of the bed beside her and hugged her close, visibly shaken.

"There's hope, Jenny," the woman finally said, untangling

herself from Jenny's arms. "The chief magistrate has already exercised judicial leniency on your behalf."

"What does that mean?" Jenny questioned, bewildered.

"I don't know the details," her aunt replied. "Except it means a delay in your being formally charged. And Jenny, were it not for this benefactor of yours, Sir Thomas would be obligated to hire attorneys and to be honest. . ."

Aunt Christine lowered her voice after a quick glance at the matron who seemed concerned only with her knitting. "We haven't the means we've sometimes led others to believe," she murmured. "I hope you understand, Jenny."

"Of course," Jenny replied in a small voice, glancing up at her aunt, who smiled faintly. Suddenly it seemed to Jenny that she was just going through the formalities until she would be. . .hanged? She felt helpless in the face of forces that seemed determined to bring her personal destruction.

"Is Uncle Thomas coming to see me?" she asked.

"He cannot even leave the house without being mobbed, Jenny. You can't imagine what a stir this has caused. And he's been so busy with the legal proceedings. As I said, these transactions are highly irregular. And now, since he is no longer your legal guardian, he may not be allowed to see you." She stood quickly, adding, "But Emmaline is waiting outside."

Aunt Christine seemed eager to get away, and Jenny couldn't blame the woman. Her aunt did kiss her cheek and say, "If you're innocent, Jenny, then you have nothing to worry about."

It was the "if" that stuck in Jenny's mind, and she was hardly aware of her aunt leaving and Emmaline entering the room until her cousin sat beside her and took her hand. Emmaline seemed sympathetic. "There are probably women all over Europe who admire you for this, Jenny. Those stuck in marriages they abhor and can do nothing about. You've probably given them ideas."

"You believe I did it, Emmaline?" Jenny asked desperately. "How can you?"

"Didn't you? Oh, Jenny, all the evidence. . ." Emmaline's voice trailed off and a pained expression appeared in her eyes.

"But the evidence shows I had everything to gain, Emmaline. A title. Great wealth. Why should I kill him?"

"Because of your views on love, Jenny. You said that wealth and titles mean nothing to you."

Jenny was momentarily flabbergasted. "You told those things to the magistrate?"

Emmaline looked guilty. "I had to, Jenny. The truth must come out at times like this."

"You yourself said you would like to see him in his grave, Emmaline."

"But that was merely an expression, Jenny."

"I know, Emmaline. That's why I didn't mention your words to the magistrate. Or how upset your parents were when Bodley asked for my hand. Or you! I would not try to implicate any of you."

Emmaline looked distressed. "Well, Jenny, if you didn't kill Ignatius, who did?"

Jenny did not reply. Emmaline stared at her for awhile, then attempted further conversation, but Jenny remained silent. Finally, Emmaline left the room. The matron closed the door behind the visitor and returned to her knitting.

Who did? Those words kept running through Jenny's mind. She had obeyed the stranger who said, "Don't mention I was here." She had not mentioned him for he seemed so far removed from such a matter. He was someone to think about when she was alone. He was the only man who had ever taken her in his arms and kissed her as if she were the most wonderful person in the world. She had felt protected and had wanted to stay in his arms forever. She had not wanted to tell those things to the magistrate.

She hadn't believed anyone would accuse her of murder. Now it was too late to say anything. To whom could she speak anyway? There was only an uncommunicative matron nearby. Anything she might say now would appear to be a made-up story and make her look either more guilty or insane. Even her own relatives had doubts about her innocence, so how could she expect strangers to believe her?

On impulse, she had given her heart to that stranger in the glade. He had said, "I will come for you tomorrow," and she had believed that. What a gudgeon she was.

That evening when it was time to retire, a guard locked the door to the room so that Jenny could not escape after the matron fell asleep. The small action made Jenny feel even more like a prisoner. She became more aware of her surroundings—the stark, bare walls, the skimpy furnishings, and the matron now lying on the cot near the door.

A chill crept over her. It would be much better to be put to death than to be thrown in a prison with even more deplorable conditions. Then she remembered the day one of the Cottingham servants had come in wide-eyed and declared, "Ah seen a mon hanged, ah did!"

Jenny had listened to the exciting details with great interest, even to the man's swinging from the gallows and the hangman pulling his feet from below to ensure the noose was tight enough to break his neck or choke the life out of him.

She pulled the blankets closer around her but could not still her shaking. She covered her head lest her chattering teeth disturb the matron. During the long night, Jenny could find no escape into her fantasies. Reality was much, much too insistent.

a

The elegance of the coach that appeared at the front door the next morning astounded Jenny. It was white, trimmed in gold, and drawn by four magnificent horses. The dour-faced matron even registered surprise as she appraised the red velvet lining of the interior—hardly the usual mode of transportation for prisoners.

An officer of the law presented official papers to the skeptical Mrs. Millet, who wore a brown woolen shawl around her shoulders. The matron was simply dressed in a dark blue skirt and muslin blouse.

Mrs. Millet's black eyes darted from the papers to the officer. "Everything seems to be in order, however odd the situation may be," she said with a skeptical lift of her eyebrows.

The officer, Mrs. Millet, and Jenny climbed inside the carriage and the officer sat opposite Jenny and the matron. His sympathetic eyes moved toward Jenny, and he spoke kindly. "Sometimes ladies are given special privilege," he said in partial explanation of the unusual turn of events.

Although they talked little, Jenny learned that the officer was a family man and had known the matron's late husband. Mr. Millet had been an officer, killed in the line of duty.

"We helped many a wayward youngster in our day, we did," Mrs. Millet assured him, and the officer nodded after a glance at Jenny and changed the subject.

The carriage sped far outside the city of London, over beautiful countryside, in the direction of Cornwall. Finally they came to a lovely village near the sea, and high atop a hill, far in the distance, gleamed a castle with golden-trimmed turrets that glistened in the sunshine.

They passed the village, where heads turned to view the magnificent carriage and horses. Jenny wondered what the villagers would say if they knew the carriage carried an accused murderess. She shuddered at the thought.

They turned onto a long winding road and traveled higher and higher, ever nearer the castle. Only after they were inside the great iron gates did Jenny speak. "That can't be a jail, can it?"

The matron looked confused. "No, it's not," she said, looking around nervously.

"Is the jail near here?" Jenny asked.

"None exists that I know of," Mrs. Millet replied, looking at the officer questioningly.

He shrugged. "Just following orders." He assured her that the other officer, riding with the coachman, was a fellow worker and a personal acquaintance of his for several years and could be trusted implicitly.

Soon the carriage stopped in front of the castle. The officer sounded the large knocker on the front door, and a butler responded. As if on cue, he was immediately flanked by footmen in uniform. Other servants lined the great foyer.

A distinguished gray-haired man, wearing a gray suit, strode from the study. Bowing low, he said, "Welcome to Withington Castle, Lady Jennifer."

Jenny curtsied, feeling quite bewildered by the unexpected turn of events. Might this be ridicule? Might it be punishment for having spent the past week being waited on by servants and attending the engagement party while, as everyone seemed to believe, she actually had a murderous heart?

This gentleman would certainly know she had no claim to be called "lady." She looked at Mrs. Millet and the officer. They appeared as puzzled as she.

The gentleman handed Mrs. Millet documents from the court, stating that, due to an appeal from the Crown, Jenny would be confined to the castle until the time a formal charge was made and she was brought to trial. The papers outlined Mrs. Millet's duties.

Jenny wondered if she would be imprisoned in the dungeon or a tower.

"Lady Jennifer," the gentleman said.

Jenny swallowed hard. It was difficult not to respond to his pleasant, courteous manner. At the same time, however, his dark gray eyes penetrated hers, as if he were trying to read her mind. He appeared to be in charge.

"I am Silas Bingham, of Bingham, Bingham, and Chadwick, attorneys-at-law," he said.

Mrs. Millet gasped audibly. Jenny had heard her uncle Thomas speak of this man. The famous Bingham, with a reputation known throughout Europe, stood before her. He did not look at all like the ogre he was portrayed to be in newspaper caricatures. He could get anyone free or convicted, depending upon his whim, they said. Few individuals, however, could afford his fees.

The officer stepped forward and bowed deeply. Silas Bingham nodded, then again turned his attention to Jenny.

"I am your attorney, My Lady, employed by the illustrious Tilden Withington, the latest duke from a long line of Withingtons who, incidentally, laid the very foundations of this castle. We," he said, making a sweeping gesture with his hand that included the retinue of servants, "are at your service."

The servants introduced themselves, bowing or curtseying, and explained their positions in the household. Jenny had never known there could be so many servants in one place, but to run a castle, she supposed it necessary.

"Might I speak with you, Sir," Jenny asked hesitantly, "before anything else?" She felt terribly self-conscious about being treated royally by servants dressed better than she. Was this a farce? Or an asylum?

Silas Bingham smiled. "I anticipated that," he said. "Please come with me."

He turned to Mrs. Millet. "I'm sure you would like to see your rooms, Mrs. Millet. The servants will show you. You will act in the capacity of chaperone to Lady Jennifer. That is a stipulation of the court."

Mrs. Millet followed the servant up the wide staircase to the south wing of the second floor.

After Bingham dismissed the officer, wishing him well on his return to London, he led Jenny to the study.

"Sit here, please." He indicated a large velvet chair near a huge marble fireplace and then sat across from her.

"You did not expect this, did you, Lady Jennifer?" he asked gently.

"No, Sir," she replied and faintly returned his smile.

"You are here by royal appeal, in the custody of His Grace, Tilden Withington. He personally approached the king, making an appeal on your behalf, which was granted. This is your home for the present."

Bingham walked over to the desk, picked up some papers, and brought them over to Jenny. "As you will see, there are official seals on the papers. Sir Thomas Cottingham has relinquished all his rights as legal guardian, and you are now the ward of Tilden Withington."

"His. . .his ward?" Jenny asked with incredulity.

"Not in the sense of your aunt and uncle," Bingham explained. "But the duke is responsible for your welfare during this period of, shall we say, confinement. He must personally escort you to London for formal charges and the trial at the proper time."

"Am I supposed to know him?" Jenny asked.

"Not necessarily," Bingham replied. He leaned back in the comfortable chair and eyed her with frank and intelligent scrutiny. "You might say he is a distant relative."

She knew of no relatives. "How does he know me?"

Silas Bingham leaned forward. "My dear Lady Jennifer," he began.

"Please call me Jenny," she requested, the title making her uncomfortable.

"Jenny," he said. "We have been searching for you since you were five years old. Since your father held legal custody of you, we could do nothing but make our report of your whereabouts. But whenever we located you, by the time our report reached the appropriate persons, you were whisked off to France, Italy, or another confounded place. His Grace has personally searched for you for several years, giving up only after you were legally placed in the custody of the Cottinghams."

Astonished, Jenny's questions tumbled forth. "Why would anyone search for me? Who is Duke Withington? Why am I in a castle with servants, when I should be in jail?" So many questions. She put her hand to her forehead, feeling she must be dreaming.

Silas Bingham spoke kindly. "We will have plenty of time to talk, Jennifer. We must prepare for the trial."

"Am I a. . .prisoner here?" she asked, thinking she would like to remain one if this were her punishment.

"As far as the court is concerned, yes. But while you are here, just ask for what you want, and it will be yours."

"Does this happen often?"

"No," Bingham replied. "Fortunately, His Grace has influential friends in royal circles."

Jenny's deep blue eyes widened. "Oh, I won't do anything to break that trust or cause him undue concern. I won't run away or anything like that. I am very grateful."

Silas Bingham nodded. "The servants know you are not to leave the grounds. They would notify the appropriate authorities immediately if that were attempted. However, you may walk or ride on the grounds. You may be almost alone, Jenny, but there will always be those to, shall we say, protect or accompany you."

"I know I must be dreaming," Jenny said.

"We will do everything in our power to make the months before the trial as comfortable as possible. The duke has ordered everyone to give you the respect and attention that you deserve. Also, if you will forgive me for mentioning such a personal issue, it is clear that you did not arrive with enough clothing for an extended stay. As His Grace's ward, you will be expected to have new gowns fashioned for your use. Our housekeeper will arrange the necessary details with you. "

Jenny blushed, but she understood the necessity of expanding her wardrobe. Aunt Christine had only brought a couple of her old dresses to her the day before. She looked across at Bingham quite suddenly. There were so many questions on the tip of her tongue, but before she could ask, Silas Bingham caught her quite off guard.

He stood, studying her with hard eyes, and asked in a stern voice, "Miss Jennifer Cottingham, are you guilty of the crime of which you are accused?"

"Oh, no," she replied, jumping to her feet, immediately placing her hand against her thundering heart. "I am innocent."

"Rum!" he exclaimed, his eyes glittering with pleasure. He went to the study doors and opened them. "We will talk tomorrow morning at nine, if that pleases you."

Jenny agreed to the appointment, then walked over and stood in front of him. The eyes she had thought were gray were actually light blue. His smile softened the lines of what had momentarily seemed quite a stern countenance. His gray hair gave him the appearance of someone's very nice father. She would never, at that moment, have believed he was known as the horror of the courts.

Bingham took her hand, lifted it to his lips, and gently kissed the back of it.

Jenny curtsied, feeling like a grand lady, although dressed in one of her plainest gowns and wearing her hair twisted into that horrid coil. She turned and saw that servants waited to escort her to her room.

It was not a room to which they took her, however, but a suite of rooms with an ancient elegance fit for a queen. Jenny gasped as she walked through the bedroom, dressing room, drawing room, private dining area, and a Roman bath that her personal maid said had been added by His Grace only the year before. There were several other baths throughout the castle.

This was a hundred times more elegant than the suite of rooms Jenny had used that terrible evening at Bodley House. Most impressive was the bedroom, aglow from the light of a dancing fire that warmed away the coolness of the spring evening.

"We thought you'd like a fire, M'Lady," the maid said as Jenny walked toward the hearth, holding out her hands to warm them. "It takes awhile for the stones to warm after a cold winter so near the sea."

Jenny smiled. "What is your name?"

"Nellie," the girl replied.

"Are you employed at the castle year-round?" Jenny asked the girl, who obviously was so eager to please her. The girl couldn't have been more than a few years younger than Jenny, and her dark eyes filled with speculation and excitement whenever she looked at her new mistress. She wore a dark blue dress with a white apron and cap.

"Not I, except upon special occasions," Nellie replied. "But my mother and father are. We live in a cottage on the castle grounds. My mother tells stories of the grand balls the old duke, God rest his soul, used to give. Ladies and gentlemen came from all around and dined by the light of hundreds of candles. Why one time, the king himself did attend." She sighed. "But that was years ago—when I was a wee babe. Then the duke sailed abroad, and he returned to England only a couple times before he died. The new duke lives at the castle now, but we only see him for a few months at a time. Most of the year he is abroad on business."

"And does he have grand parties?" Jenny asked excitedly, eager to learn any bit of information about this mysterious situation and the Withington family.

"He hasn't thrown any grand parties," Nellie replied,

hanging the last of Jenny's plain gowns in the closet. She turned toward her, adding, "But he has attended them. He did, of course, receive a personal invitation from the king when he threw that private birthday party." Nellie covered her mouth with her hand. "Oh, but I've said too much. My family has been loyal to the dukes for many generations. We will be loyal to you, as well."

Perhaps, Jenny thought, she and the Withingtons could trust Nellie and her family to be loyal. And yet, Jenny knew she was providing Nellie with the kind of personal story that would be talked about for generations to come. Although loyal, the servant girl would tell her children and grandchildren that she had been a personal maid to an accused murderess who was, for awhile, treated like a grand lady in the castle before she was. . .what? Released? Hanged?

Shivering, Jenny moved closer to the fire.

Nellie took extra quilts from a closet and spread them across the bed. "You will need these during the night."

Jenny's wish to dine alone in her suite was granted. She didn't want to take the offered hospitality so far as to sit in a formal room and have servants cater to her every whim. Deep inside, she feared some kind of mockery underfoot, like giving a convicted man a sumptuous meal before snuffing the life out of him. Why was she being given this taste of heaven? Was it a sign of impending, inevitable doom? Did her gracious benefactor suspect that her young life was near an end and feel pity for her?

The dining area in Jenny's suite looked too lonely with its view of the nighttime darkness, so Jenny chose to sit in front of the fire in the bedroom. She hardly noticed what kinds of food she was served, but realizing she was quite hungry, she ate it all.

After a long, sublime soaking in a tub filled with warm water and fragrant with a scent that Nellie had added, Jenny slipped into a comfortable nightgown. Then she propped up on fluffy pillows at the head of the half-canopy bed and tried to concentrate on Jane Austen's *Mansfield Park,* a book she'd asked Nellie to bring from the library.

Apparently satisfied that Jenny had everything that she needed, Nellie blew out the candles in the wall niches and curtsied at the door. "Mrs. Millet told me to remind you that she is directly across the hall, should you need her for anything," she said before leaving.

Jenny suspected that this message was Mrs. Millet's method of reminding her that she was a prisoner. Whether Silas Bingham labeled her a chaperone, companion, or guest of the castle, Mrs. Millet remained an employee of the court, and the legal papers stipulated that she remain in the castle with Jenny.

Unable to concentrate on the book, Jenny laid it on the bedside table and blew out the candles. The fire burned low, and Jenny pulled the covers closer to her chin and closed her eyes, suddenly aware of an overwhelming need for sleep.

She didn't know what awakened her during the night. For long minutes, she lay perfectly still, listening. An eerie wind from the sea rattled the windows, and from somewhere along the castle wall came the sound of something scratching the stone.

Outside, the moonlight threw trees into silhouettes against the silk curtains at her window. The limbs stretched toward her and seemed to be reaching inside the room, down onto the floor, and across the bed. The moving shadows crept along the walls, turning the niches into dark caverns and the fireplace into a black forbidden hole. The carved ceiling changed into monstrous images. Even the half-canopy woven in rich colors of blue, red, and gold velvet showed only varying shades of gray. The protective bed curtains now resembled arms, hovering, waiting.

With an exclamation of fear, Jenny bolted upright in bed,

threw back the covers, and stepped out onto the floor. With shaking fingers, she lighted the candles on the bedside table. Immediately the leaping flames dispelled the shadows, and a golden glow once again played about the room and across the stone walls.

An illusion, Jenny told herself, with a sigh of relief. No encroaching evil lurked to overtake her. But while the shadows and the wind held no threat, evil was present in the world. Its nearness to her was no illusion. She trembled.

Jenny sat on the edge of her bed, staring at cold ashes where a warm fire had burned several hours before. Over the past three days, one question continued to plague her: Who killed Lord Bodley?

Suppose she had run away before the engagement party? Would Bodley have been murdered? Was it someone angry about the engagement? She shut her eyes against the possibility of the evil deed being committed by one of the Cottinghams, her only relatives. She was ashamed to even consider such a possibility.

The magistrate had implied the action was that of an unthinking, distraught female. But had she premeditated murder, wouldn't she also have had the presence of mind to attempt to cover her tracks? She would not have left a glass of poison on a table. Even if she'd heard people coming, she would have thrown the goblet into the trees where it would have been more difficult to find.

Only two other ladies were in the glade, according to witnesses. Suppose, just suppose, Aunt Christine had been upset enough to eliminate Bodley. Jenny shook her head disparagingly and sighed. She could not envision Aunt Christine leaving a glass with poison on the table. The woman would have had greater presence of mind in such a situation.

What about Emmaline? Jenny's cousin could be impulsive, even irrational at times, but of course her rash acts had never approached something this drastic. Emmaline was the type to plan an action without thought to the consequences. But a murder?

Jenny reproached herself for even considering that her cousin could be capable of such an act. Yet the fact remained: Someone had murdered Lord Bodley. The magistrates had accused Jenny. Why had they not felt Emmaline's motives were greater than her own? It was Emmaline who had been jilted. It was to Aunt Christine's great humiliation that Bodley had chosen Jenny instead of Emmie.

Had social standing influenced the magistrates? Why did she look more like a killer than her relatives? Had the Cottingham family plotted to avenge their embarrassment and place the blame on Jenny? Is that why Emmaline had told the investigators that Jenny had made a threat against Bodley's life? Or did Uncle Thomas and Aunt Christine suspect that Emmaline might have committed the act? Were they trying to steer the blame away from their daughter?

"I don't know," Jenny whispered in the darkness.

Or did an answer exist—one that she simply refused to accept?

five

Jenny awoke with a start at the sounds of heavy knocking on the door and of Nellie frantically calling her name. By the time Jenny opened the door, Mrs. Millet had hurried from her room, tying the sash of her heavy robe. Her flushed face and anxious eyes indicated grave concern.

Jenny realized they thought she might have harmed herself. Strange, that had not occurred to her. And yet, wouldn't that be the simplest, most natural way out of an unbearable situation?

Jenny knew if she took such drastic action, it would look as if Mrs. Millet had shirked her official duty, and Nellie would feel that she had failed the dukes whom her family had served for generations.

Nellie began to fuss about Jenny, straightening her bed, asking if she wanted her breakfast in her room, could she draw another bath, or was there anything at all she might do for her.

Jenny asked about riding horses and within the hour sat atop a chestnut mare with which she had a delightful affinity from the onset. Garbed in her simple but adequate riding outfit, she followed a groom, who offered to show her the most desired route to take, instructing her which path from the woods led into the open countryside and which led to dangerous cliffs above the sea.

As soon as they emerged from the wooded path, Jenny felt the open spaces beckon to her. With the groom ahead of her, and another servant a respectful distance behind, she quelled the temptation to ride on forever. The early morning adventure proved to be invigorating, and much of her tension evaporated like the dew upon the spring grass once it is touched by the gentle rays of morning sun.

Wanting the grooms to know she could be trusted not to leave the grounds, nor to gallop at a high rate of speed and throw herself over the cliffs and into the sea, Jenny kept her emotions in tight rein. The mare sensed and respected her wishes. Jenny suspected her mount would have been happier to be swept away in a fast gallop, and she herself thought such a ride would provide a wonderful escape from life's concerns.

But Jenny was extremely grateful for even a small amount of diversion from the matters pressing on her mind. However, she knew she had to return to the stables for her appointment with Bingham must neither be missed nor delayed.

A short while later, Jenny had bathed and enjoyed the light breakfast Nellie had brought to her room. Promptly at nine o'clock, Jenny descended to the study, where she met Bingham, who was sitting at the huge mahogany desk.

Jenny's blue eyes sparkled with excitement as she related to Bingham the enjoyment of her morning ride on the chestnut mare. Bingham delighted in her asking him to ride with her in the mornings.

"Thank you, gracious lady," he responded with apparently genuine admiration. "That would be delightful, but there is much work to do, and so little time in which to do it."

With that, their conversation turned to the serious matter at hand. Bingham's next words astounded Jenny. "Your mother is concerned about your situation."

"That cannot be," Jenny stammered, her eyes wide in confusion. "My mother is dead."

"Why do you think your mother is dead, Jennifer?"

Jenny noticed that his face revealed no shock at her claim. She clasped her hands on her lap and leaned toward Bingham, while he took notes. Her heart seemed about to flutter out of her chest. Her weak and shaky voice answered his question. "My father," she said. "He told me that my mother died. Uncle Thomas and Aunt Christine never refuted that."

"Your mother is alive. At present she is mourning the loss of her husband. She is in America. That is where Tilden has gone. To fetch her."

Jenny could scarcely breathe. Her mother, of whom she had heard such terrible stories and whom she had thought quite dead, was really alive. "How can I believe these things?" Jenny said. "Why would Tilden Withington fetch her? I don't understand."

"You have never heard of the Withingtons before coming here, Jenny?"

She paused to consider his question. "No, Sir," she replied, wondering why she would be expected to know the family.

"You've never heard the name of the man your mother ran away with?"

"Only that he was a duke," Jenny replied.

Silas Bingham shook his gray head. "The duke was Stanford Withington, Jenny."

Jenny stared at him wide-eyed. It was difficult to take it all in. Quite impossible, really.

"Duke Stanford died over a year ago," Bingham said.

"But you said my mother is in mourning."

A distressed look passed over Bingham's eyes. "Yes, Jenny, I did." He cleared his throat before continuing. "The loss of Duke Stanford has been almost more than Lady Diane can bear. She and the duke sacrificed everything because of their love for each other."

Even her child? Jenny wondered.

"You can well understand, I am sure," he continued, "how the two of them would cling to each other so entirely, having lost so much else. Stanford's title became virtually ineffective because of his living in America. You well know the reputation of a woman who leaves her husband. She becomes a woman scorned, an outcast of society, publicly ostracized, regardless of private opinion. 'Ladies,' " he said, emphasizing the word, "would not be allowed to associate with her."

Jenny lowered her head to hide her expression from Bingham. Another illusion shattered. Running away with the man she loved had not brought her mother all the happiness she had sought.

"You know nothing of your mother, Jennifer?" Silas Bingham asked kindly.

Saddened, she shook her head. "My aunt said we would never discuss my mother under her roof. But she often remarked that I would turn out to be like my mother. She did not mean it kindly."

"Tell me about it, Jenny," Bingham encouraged gently. "Not just the facts, but your feelings and impressions. As far back as you can remember."

Jenny paused to gather her thoughts. Then she explained to Bingham how her early recollections were hazy. There seemed to be a time when she was happy and felt secure and loved. Then she had a recurring dream. She was in a small enclosure, like a pantry. She had been very sleepy, but frightened, and made a sound. A hand came over her mouth. She could not scream, and because she began to cry, her nose stopped up and she could scarcely breathe.

Afterward she'd been taken to her room and had called for her mother, but she never saw her mother again. Then her life became a steady succession of new homes, moving from one place to another, one country to another, with her father.

When old enough, she began to ask why she had no mother. "Is she in heaven?" the little Jenny had asked.

"No, she is not in heaven. Now get out of my sight," her father would reply in a drunken rage. "You have no mother. The sooner you realize that, the better off you will be."

Jenny had learned to talk with him only when he was sober, which was seldom. Often he would moan, "I have no friends; money comes only by selling my possessions; and it's all because of that. . ." Then he would refer to Jenny's mother in very vulgar terms.

When he made such accusations against her mother, Jenny would run and hide and put her hands over her ears to keep out the words. She pretended her mother would come and rescue her.

Her father went away for long periods of time, leaving Jenny in the care of a series of governesses. Some of the young women were terrible bores. Others were extremely intelligent and sensitive. They talked to Jenny about life and tried to make her understand that her father drank because he was heartbroken that he had no wife and she had no mother. They introduced her to books, and in them she found a sense of security.

There had been no time for close attachments. She'd been sad when they had to leave a place and those she loved. She seemed forever trying to find her mother in each new governess, each new servant.

Jenny had always longed for her father to return. When he was drinking, he wanted nothing to do with her. When he wasn't, he sometimes embraced her.

When Jenny reached the age of twelve, her governesses began to be of poorer quality. They did not know as much as she had gleaned from her books, always hoping to impress her father with her knowledge. Jenny pretended that each new place, whether in Russia, France, or Scotland, would be her permanent home. She made attempts to learn each country's language and history. Her father gave her a new name in each place they lived.

"I don't even know if Jenny is my real name. Do you know?" she asked Bingham.

"Yes," Bingham replied. "Your real name is Sarah Jennifer Greenough."

"Cottingham," Jenny finished.

"No," Bingham replied. "You were never legally adopted by the Cottinghams. They had you take on their name so no one would know you were a Greenough. Your father was Sir William Greenough, the brother of your aunt Christine Greenough Cottingham."

Jenny leaned back, expectantly waiting for some kind of explanation to help fill the vacant spots in her life. She knew so little. And now, looking back on it, it seemed her father and she had been hiding or running from someone or something.

"Our hands were tied," Bingham said. "Your father had legal custody of you, and when we found you or the place of your father's residence, we could only report to Duke Stanford. However, your father believed that Duke Stanford would whisk you away upon the first opportunity, which is exactly what the duke had in mind."

The duke wanted to kidnap her? For her mother? It was almost more than Jenny could do not to interrupt Bingham and ask the numerous questions whirling around in her head.

"Sometimes your father returned to his houses and sold the furniture and paintings," Bingham said. "But you were never with him. You were thirteen when your father died," he went on. "We didn't know that for awhile, for he had been living under an alias. When we did learn of his passing, we couldn't do anything legally, for so many years had passed since his death and your father had signed papers, giving the Cottinghams legal custody of you. Our office contacted Sir Thomas as soon as we discovered your father had died, but we could not reach you personally with your mother's letters."

Jenny gasped. "My mother tried to reach me? I never knew that."

Bingham threw his pen down on the papers piled neatly on

the desk and with great vigor pushed his chair back and jumped to his feet. He paced the floor, obviously disgruntled. "Ah, if only foresight were as obvious as hindsight," he said fiercely.

After taking a deep breath, he continued calmly. "Sir Thomas had complete charge of all your father's holdings. In spite of the fact that your father died from drinking too much alcohol, he had insight enough to draw up a contract, giving your aunt and uncle complete control of any assets he had. They would become your legal guardian and were to insure that you received further education and were given a substantial amount of money each year."

"I was allowed to be tutored along with Emmaline," Jenny said in her aunt and uncle's defense, not mentioning that she had already known most of the material. She had never lacked for enough to eat. "I didn't think my father had very much money when he died."

"He had most of it invested in property and some in banks. It was simply that a couple of years before his death he apparently stopped caring about anything but gambling and drinking."

"I never knew my mother was alive. There were never any letters for me," Jenny said with a desolate note in her voice.

"We suspected as much," Bingham replied. "The Cottinghams kept a close watch on you so that none of our spies could get near enough to even speak with you. Lady Diane's letters returned unopened. Then your aunt wrote that you detested your mother and wanted no contact with her."

Jenny could only shake her head. "I wish your office or someone could have made contact with me," she said sincerely. "I've always wanted to be with my mother."

Bingham nodded. "Until you went to live with the Cottinghams, Lady Diane wanted us to find you so that Tilden could kidnap you. Of course our own office could have no part in such an action."

"And after the Cottinghams took me in?" Jenny asked.

"Eight years had passed, Jenny, since you had had any contact with your mother. We all knew it was too late for a kidnaping of a thirteen-year-old girl. Lady Diane believed your life at the Cottinghams would be a reasonably happy one, but she wanted you to know she loved you. Although she suspected someone else was responsible for her letters being returned unopened and for the notes declaring that you wanted no contact with her, she believed that you might bear resentment against her."

With a great sigh, Silas Bingham returned to his chair. "Over a year ago," he said, "Duke Stanford Withington died of a fever he contracted during an epidemic. He never gave up hope of reuniting you and your mother. His brother, Tilden, who spent his time in both America and England, managed much of Stanford's business affairs. Tilden is extremely fond of Lady Diane. Through the years, he has been obsessed with the idea of finding you and returning you to her. As he grew older, and you grew older, the idea had to be abandoned, of course. Then after Stanford's death, Tilden could not leave Lady Diane's side for many months. She was utterly bereft. In recent months, Tilden has again become determined to find you. He promised your mother he would force you to see her, to let her explain things to you. He promised to do that even if he had to take you by force."

Jenny's surprised eyes met Bingham's. "He. . .sounds very determined."

"Yes, he is," Bingham said and smiled. "He would do anything to reunite you and your mother. He has been greatly touched by her suffering all these years."

Jenny looked down. Duke Tilden must love her mother. She wondered if he would now step into his brother's place in her mother's heart. Her mother must be an easy person to love.

"What is my mother like? How does she look? Why did she abandon me? How could she?" The questions poured forth.

Bingham stood. "Those are questions Lady Diane must answer, Jenny. You and I must be about the business of saving you from the gallows."

Jenny stood and wrapped her arms around herself to hide the shudder that traveled through her frame. Preoccupied with the news about her mother, she had forgotten that horrible indictment hanging over her head.

Bingham looked at the watch he took from his vest pocket. "I have an appointment, Jenny, and will be away during the weekend. I will return around ten o'clock on Monday morning."

He stepped forward and grasped her by the shoulders. "I know it will take awhile for you to absorb what I've told you this morning. But I want you to think carefully about this horrible accusation that has been made against you. When I return, we must go over every detail of this affair, omitting nothing."

❧

Over the next couple days, Jenny came to realize that life at the castle would have been perfect if she didn't have an accusation of murder hanging over her head. She was grateful when Mrs. Millet, somewhat at a loss over what to do, struck up a friendship with Nellie's mother, the head housekeeper. Jenny was careful not to speak frankly about anything personal to anyone, for Bingham had warned her that one could never be sure when words might be misconstrued, as had her exaggerated remarks about wanting Bodley dead.

Most of the castle had been closed off and not used for many years, Nellie told Jenny, as she unlocked the door to the picture gallery with keys her mother had loaned her. The walls were lined with paintings of generations of Withingtons and their duchesses—all lovely, elegant women, each with a look of strong will and determination in their expressive eyes.

There were no paintings of Duke Stanford, nor of her mother, for they had spent their married life in America rather than at the castle. Nor were there any of the present Duke Tilden.

"This is Duke Stanford and Duke Tilden's father," Nellie explained. "My mother described him as a terror to his enemies, but a wonderfully straightforward and fair man toward those he liked and trusted."

"Did he die in battle?" Jenny asked.

"Oh, no," Nellie replied. "He spent most of his younger years fighting for the king. My mother says women were wild for him, but he did not marry until well into his forties. These paintings were done by a very famous artist shortly following the wedding of the elderly duke Withington and his young bride, whom he loved dearly. My mother said," Nellie continued, "that the dukes always had a rather wild streak in them, and could not settle down until their adventurous nature had been abated. She called it a thirst for blood, and said it was only too marvelous that the king needed men like that in his service—otherwise all the dukes would have been atrocious villains."

Jenny smiled, while staring at the painting of the earlier Duke Withington, while in his forties. He was a strong, incredibly handsome man, and his penetrating eyes bore into hers from the painting. She thought he could subdue an enemy with a single glance. Yet a rather rakish look about him reminded her of the stranger in the glade.

Having seen enough, Jenny turned to leave the gallery. She did not wish to think of the stranger in the glade. She should forget that he ever existed, as he apparently had forgotten her. She often wondered if he had been real or simply a figment of her imagination.

That night, however, she dreamed of the stranger who had

held her in his arms and kissed her. He appeared as some kind of hero who promised to rescue her from an impending, disastrous marriage. Then she awakened in a cold sweat, as if, even in her dreams, she would not allow those additional, threatening, excruciatingly painful thoughts into her mind.

On Monday morning, during her consultation with Bingham, Jenny had to face the facts.

"You are holding something back," he said. "You must not do that but must tell me everything, no matter how insignificant it may seem."

"It will not be believed and will make me appear foolish or deranged," she replied.

"No matter," he assured. "It is my job to help you, not condemn you. But you must trust me. Now out with it, Child."

Jenny told him about the stranger. Bingham's penetrating stare compelled her to tell him everything, from the words they said to the kisses they shared. "I was just young and foolish and frightened," she said, hoping that would be a suitable explanation for her actions. "Do you believe me?"

"I believe you," Bingham replied. "There were two glasses in the glade. Young ladies do not ordinarily go about after dinner with goblets in their hands. I had known all along there must be someone else, but your not telling me that could well imply that you are guilty and had an accomplice."

"Oh, Mr. Bingham, you don't think I'm guilty?" Her voice choked, and she felt close to tears. She could almost think of this man as a loving father, were it not that she had allowed the absent Duke Tilden Withington to occupy that space in her mind and heart. And Bingham had often told her that their relationship must remain somewhat formal so that he could be completely objective.

"This is difficult," he had said once, "because you are so beautiful and as sweet a girl I would want my own daughter to be, if I had one." He did not, however, but had one son, Edgar

Bingham, a partner in the law firm. "I do have a granddaughter. And a mighty fine one," he had added upon that rare time when he spoke personally.

Now he was speaking of the stranger. "Was he a rogue and a rake sort of fellow?"

"Oh, no," Jenny replied immediately. "He was definitely a gentleman. The finest looking man I have ever seen. He looked exquisite in his formal evening clothes, and his cravat was tied to perfection. Apparently he was very wealthy, for I feel certain that was a diamond pin he wore on the cravat, and he wore rings with jewels on his fingers."

Her heart beat faster just remembering the stranger who had kissed her and her ardent response. Now she looked down at her fingers. "But one cannot tell by outward appearance, can one?" she added in a small voice.

When Bingham did not answer, she finally looked over to find a contemplative expression in his eyes. "The thing we have to discover, Jenny," he said distantly, "is not only that you did not murder Lord Bodley, but we have to discover who did."

Jenny rose from the chair. She walked around the room, touching objects, looking at paintings on the walls, gazing into the fireplace where no fire glowed. Emmaline had asked once, "If you didn't kill him, Jenny, then who did?"

"Maybe he killed himself," she said now. "He knew I didn't love him and never would. Perhaps he realized how hopeless—" Her words stopped in the face of Silas Bingham's slowly shaking head.

"Bodley did not commit suicide," he said gently. "Someone murdered him."

Jenny spread her hands helplessly and turned her back on Silas Bingham again.

"We will talk more tomorrow," he said finally. "Edgar will be here this afternoon to discuss the case with me."

For the rest of the day, Jenny tried to dismiss the question of who had murdered Bodley. The answer, however, appeared in the form of a dream. The stranger held her, kissed her, and spoke beautiful words of love. Then his countenance changed, and in a violent temper he struck Lord Bodley about the head. He became a monster, and Jenny awakened screaming.

Mrs. Millet could not console her, nor could Nellie, but the poor girl stayed near Jenny's bed until her sobs and shaking subsided.

Jenny could not bring herself to tell Mr. Bingham of such a dream. It seemed impossible that the stranger, who had awakened in her the first stirrings of love, could be a murderer. And yet, it also seemed impossible that she herself could be accused of murder, and that had happened.

Her affection for the stranger slowly began to be transferred to the unseen Duke Tilden Withington. As the days passed, the dreams of the monstrous stranger became less frequent, less violent. Now she dreamed of the elderly Withington, the fatherly figure who was bringing her mother back into her life.

She continued to question Bingham about her mother, but he would tell her little. "That must come from your mother," he insisted repeatedly.

"Did she not love me?" she asked.

"Your mother loved you more than anything in the world, Jenny. And you were not abandoned in the sense you have been led to believe. She has spent all these years suffering over the loss of you. The letters stating you wanted nothing to do with her simply broke her heart. She gave up hope after Duke Stanford died. That is when Tilden promised he would find you and force you to have a confrontation with your mother."

"Will she come?" Jenny asked.

"She will come," Bingham replied. But on the question of when, he remained silent.

six

Finally the day arrived. Jenny's mother had been ill during the voyage and begged to become more presentable before seeing Jenny. Bingham said, however, that the duke would receive Jenny within the half hour.

Jenny washed her face, flushed with excitement. Her blue eyes sparkled.

Would the duke be pleased with her? Would he like to have a girl like her for a daughter?

She repaired a few curls that hung way past her shoulders and brought several forward to lie against the front of her dress. Her black hair contrasted beautifully with the deep rose-colored gown which showed her trim figure to advantage. Tiny pink rosebuds graced the front of the fashionable gown and her waist was naturally slim. She'd had the gown made for the particular occasion of coming face-to-face with the duke who was making her lifelong dream of meeting her mother a reality.

Only for an instant did Jenny think of the stranger in the glade. She admitted to herself that it had been he who caused her present distressful predicament. She had been foolish to think she had fallen in love with the stranger. It was simply that the men in her life, other than Bodley, had been limited to. . .zero.

Now, a different kind of man had come into her life. One who had unselfishly devoted months and years of his life to reuniting a mother and daughter. She loved him for that and would be eternally grateful. She admired and respected the man who had sent her to his home, used his influence with royal personages to keep her from jail, and had her treated like a lady. Perhaps she would be executed or banished for the crime of murder. But until that time, she would be brave. She would earn the respect of Duke Tilden Withington.

Before the half hour ended, Jenny tapped on the study door, wondering which sound was louder—the knock or the pounding of her heart.

Silas Bingham opened the door. "Come in, Jenny, and meet Duke Tilden Withington," he said. After she stepped through the doorway, Bingham entered the hallway, closing the study door behind him.

Jenny looked at the floor in front of her feet lest she stumble and fall. The figure of a man moved toward her. With bowed head, she curtsied low. Duke Tilden Withington bowed.

She lifted her eyes to his. Her words of heartfelt gratitude stuck in her throat. "Y…you!" she stammered. Her mouth would not close, nor her eyes. Her heart no longer thudded against her chest, for it apparently had ceased to beat.

He was no middle-aged, fatherly figure of a man. Instead, she faced the most handsome, rakish-looking man, with delight twinkling in his eyes and a half smile gracing his lips. His eyes took in her appearance, and she blushed at what appeared to be his unmitigated admiration.

He should like her attire, she told herself. After all, hadn't he left orders that she should have whatever she wished? She had thought nothing of accepting such a generous gesture from her mother's wonderful friend. Now, she realized that he had financed every stitch of clothing she wore, just as Bodley had furnished her with silks, satins, laces, and servants.

Her experience with Bodley had led to disastrous events. Now, Jenny felt even more naïve and gullible. A sense of helplessness stole over her. She quickly glanced around the room and turned her head toward the door, seeking some escape. But no escape existed. What force had sought her out to torture and twist her young life into such knots of confusion and hopeless, unavoidable disaster?

The two men in her life were indeed one: Duke Tilden Withington was both her beloved stranger in the glade and the murderer in her nightmares.

The shocked, bewildered, even fearful expression on Jenny's face was not what Tilden had longed for. "You did not expect me?" His voice almost failed, for he stood so close to her. The fragrance of wild roses assailed his nostrils.

"No," she finally managed to gasp, taking a step back.

This was not the encounter he had expected. Until he had observed Jenny at her engagement party and then spoken with her in the glade, he had never found a love so binding as that shared by his brother, Stanford, and Lady Diane. But Tilden knew, from the very first moment, that he would never allow Jenny to become a victim of Ignatius Bodley's lewd and vile character, an infamous topic in society's circles.

After many years of indulgence, Tilden had committed himself to Christian living. He repented of his past and allowed the Spirit of the living Jesus to abide in his heart. It wasn't the easy way, but he knew it to be the best way. He'd longed for one woman's love to fill his life. He'd never found such a woman until his encounter in that shady glade with Jennifer. This sweet, wonderful girl had tempted him beyond any of the experienced women he had known in past years. Her eagerness for love and affection tore his emotions. The remembrance of her soft and yielding lips against his own haunted his dreams. Since then, any thoughts of romancing a woman had been accompanied by the image of the lovely Jenny.

For many years his top priority had been to find and kidnap Jenny for her mother. As they all grew older, managing at least a confrontation between mother and daughter had become his obsession. Now that he had encountered Jenny in person, had held her warm and tender body in his arms, he knew that he needed Jenny for himself and would be satisfied with nothing less.

But now Jenny—the girl who had been in his heart and mind so many years, the young woman he'd finally found after so many years of wondering and searching—was accused of murder. Surely they would not hang such a one as young Jenny.

Was the thought of a hanging what caused Jenny's present discomfort and fear? He could only surmise that the accusation of murder had disoriented her. How could it be otherwise? That, and that alone, must be why she gazed at him with fear in her eyes.

He deliberately spoke softly. "I told you I would come for you. However," he said, turning toward a chair and motioning for her to sit, "due to the unexpected turn of events, my coming was delayed."

"I. . .don't understand," Jenny whispered. Near to fainting, she sat in the chair, not taking her eyes from him as he lowered himself into a chair across from her.

Her heart and mind had become such foreign creatures of late, for even in this crisis she could not help but be aware of how devastatingly attractive he looked in his formal dinner clothes—the champagne-colored pantaloons and darker coat. The white lace of his shirt was in evidence at his wrists and throat. Yet she remembered Nellie's comment about the blood-thirsty Withingtons. This man had promised to take her away from all her misery. How had he succeeded in doing that? Could her rescuer also be the murderer?

Jenny had read of characters who accused a murderer to his face, and in so doing ensured their own doom. She mustn't do that. She must remember what she had learned years ago— that she must live by her wits, not by trusting or counting on anyone else.

With that resolve, she moved her hand to her slender

throat, swallowed convulsively for a moment, then breathed deeply. "I'm. . .I'm sorry," she stammered. "This is a shock."

Tilden rose quickly from the chair and walked to a closet along the far wall, near the desk where Mr. Bingham had sat so often during the past weeks while he and Jenny discussed the case. "It's quite unbelievable that Bingham has not told you of my identity," he said, opening the doors. He took out two crystal goblets and poured tonic water in each.

"Your name, yes," she replied, her voice slightly stronger. "But you did not tell me your name that night. I had no idea who you were."

He stood over her, holding out the glass. Their fingers touched as she reached for it, and her voice lowered to a whisper as she finished her thought. "Or even if you were real."

Their eyes met and neither said anything. Jenny felt as if his gaze penetrated her, and a strange tingling began to fill her being. She did not want to think that the two men she loved were one and the same. Love? No, she mustn't love him for many, many reasons. Feeling fear gathering in her throat again, she lowered her eyes and gulped the tonic water, then coughed.

Although concerned for Jenny's well-being, Tilden noticed the color in her cheeks and thought it most becoming. Naturally she was upset, having no idea he was the man she had met in the glade. She must have had some very hard thoughts about a man who would kiss and run, then be such a coward as to never show his face again. She must have thought him a bit of a rip, and of no higher moral character than Ignatius Bodley. That is, if she had thought of him at all.

"You are the girl I have been looking for since you were five years old," Tilden said, in a reminiscent tone.

Jenny raised her eyes to his. Noting her interest, Tilden continued. "I was in on the plans the night your mother and my brother slipped away to board the ship to America. I witnessed their sorrow, even felt it myself, that you were not with us." He shook his head sadly, feeling deeply the experiences of the past. "Lady Diane's suffering touched my heart."

Jenny leaned forward to hear the story. "What happened that night?"

Tilden hesitated, turning the glass in his fingers. "I think it best if Lady Diane tells you about that. It is very personal." He smiled suddenly. "The important thing is," he said softly, "that I found you."

Jenny's heart began to race again, and she almost forgot the terrible suspicions she had harbored against the stranger. "Then you were looking for me when you came to the party?" She recalled how he had been staring at her no matter where she stood in Bodley's house.

"Yes," Tilden said, his gaze penetrating. " 'I have finally found her,' I kept saying to myself. I had not seen you since I was fifteen and you were five. I had taken a message to your mother, and you had stood at the door, holding onto her skirts. Your small face seemed to be all eyes, blue and inquisitive, as you stared up at me."

"You remembered me for all those years?" Jenny asked in wonder.

"I remembered you as a child," he replied. "But when I saw you at Bodley's, I recognized you instantly. You were so like your mother when she was your age. You even had the same kind of brave sadness about you that Lady Diane had when she was married to your father and then again when she lost you."

Jenny's heart lifted at his words. Her mother had not deliberately abandoned her as she had been led to believe. Tears came to her eyes. "Now you have reunited us," she said softly. For the moment, her thoughts were most congenial toward Duke Withington, her kindly benefactor.

"It is something I have long looked forward to," he replied.

Jenny smiled, feeling a warmth from him that she had never experienced before. It was all-encompassing and much like the feeling she had experienced in the glade when he had kissed her—as if they were the only two people in the world.

Tilden saw the gratitude in her eyes, the tender expression in the most beautiful face he'd ever seen. He longed to touch her raven curls and to taste the sweet lips beneath his. The temptation was almost more than he could bear.

A pink flush graced her cheeks, and he wondered how often, if ever, she thought of their kiss. Or had she dismissed it as she had that night: simply a desperate attempt to create a pleasant memory to cling to after marriage to Ignatius Bodley? And to think, that night he had been amused when she had said she would do anything to get out of the situation.

Tilden suddenly stood and walked over to the fireplace. He propped one foot on the hearth and rested an arm on the mantle. "Have you been. . ." He started to say "happy," but one awaiting trial for murder could hardly be happy. He began again. "Have you been pleased with your surroundings?"

"Oh, Duke Withington," Jenny began, moving forward to sit on the edge of the chair.

"Tilden," he interrupted, slightly irritated with her formality.

"Tilden," she said in a small voice.

"Yes, Jenny?" he questioned, and she could no longer meet his eyes. They were so penetrating, and made her want to rush into his arms and tell him of her love. This man, who had thought of her for at least sixteen years, had approached the king on her behalf, acquired Mr. Bingham for her defense, established her in a majestic castle, and reunited her with her mother—this man could not possibly be a murderer. She refused to consider Nellie's comment about how adept the Withingtons were at eliminating their enemies.

Instead, she would now say the words she had originally planned to say upon entering the study. "You have made me the happiest girl in the world, considering my circumstances. This is a most beautiful place. You have given me more than I should dare ask for." She could not say all he had given her. A first kiss. A first love. An awakening to her own being.

"In addition to all that," she continued, "you brought my mother to me." She paused and looked up at him. "How can I ever thank you?" she asked softly.

He stared at her for a long time. She shifted her gaze, rose from the chair, and turned her back to him while taking a final sip of the tonic water and then setting the glass on the table by the chair. She inhaled deeply and walked around the room, pretending to look at the paintings. Then she stood by the window.

Jenny parted the white silk panels, flanked by gold velvet curtains, and realized that darkness approached. That wasn't all. The carpet muted his steps, but she felt his nearness. If he took her in his arms, she would be helpless to resist. More than anything at that moment, she wanted to be in his arms. It seemed, with the shadow of death hanging over her, everything in life had become so precious—the fragrance of a flower on a spring morning, a cool breeze, a ride on the chestnut mare. Even her fantasies became more meaningful, for she wanted to experience life and all its joys, not just its heartaches.

She turned to face him. Her eyes traveled along the lace ruffles on his shirt, past his throat, along his strong square jawline, and lingered momentarily upon his full lips that parted with his audible intake of breath. Then her eyes met his, and she felt mesmerized, having no will of her own. Such intense emotions in conflict with deeper instincts tugging at her consciousness warned her of danger and caused her great pain.

As he bent his head toward her pink, softly parted lips, Tilden glimpsed her troubled expression. Rather than take advantage of the situation, he cradled her in his arms, acutely aware of her. She had asked how she might repay him. He mustn't exploit her sense of gratitude by implying he sought his rewards in the same manner as the likes of Ignatius Bodley. Might she mistake his ardor for the kind of lust that she so resented in Bodley?

He should not reveal the depths of his feelings for her while so many serious matters weighed heavily upon this household. One issue, and one only, must be uppermost in their minds until this horrendous affair was settled.

Realizing how tightly he held her close, he released her, then deliberately turned and sat on the side of the heavy desk, his hands grasping the edges for support. He watched as Jenny returned to the high-backed arm chair in which she had sat a short while ago. Did she wonder why he had let her go? Or did she wonder why he had held her at all? She bowed her head to focus upon her hands, clasped demurely against the rose-pink of her dress. There was only one subject he must discuss with her at this moment.

"Jenny," he said.

She lifted her deep blue eyes to his. Was it some mysterious emotion of her own that brought into them that guarded expression, or was it simply the natural dimness of the room affected by the fading light of day?

"Jenny," he said her name again. "When I saw you so distressed over the prospect of marrying Bodley, it brought back the agony Lady Diane had lived through. I know the results of a loveless marriage, Jenny. I could not bear that happening to you. The moment I saw you, my heart went out to you. I knew I would go to any lengths to prevent your marriage to Bodley."

Jenny shivered, knowing what he meant. Tilden was forcing her to believe what she so desperately wanted not to believe. He had killed Bodley to prevent her marriage. Her initial suspicions had been correct. Her dreams had accurately identified the murderer. But she was the accused. Grateful now for the near darkness, she asked, "Do you think I will be convicted?"

When he reached out for her, she drew back so suddenly, he quickly withdrew to his original position at the desk edge. "I will do everything in my power to prevent such a thing. Silas Bingham is the finest attorney in all of Europe, perhaps the world. Oh, Jenny, Jenny. I cannot bear to even think of such a thing. We will do, are doing, everything possible to prevent that."

Jenny searched his face, now in shadows. "Suppose it's not enough?" she whispered. Would he take the blame then? Would it be too late? Her body trembled with desperation.

"It must be," Tilden said, his voice deep with emotion. "It must be enough."

Jenny saw him move like a shadow, as if coming near her. She stood quickly and stepped around to the other side of the chair, as if it would fend him off should he pounce.

The movement of his head and his outstretched hand in the now-darkened room seemed so much like her nightmares. All the horrible things she had refused to admit were coming true. Each time something good and beautiful came to her, it turned out to be an illusion, bringing sure destruction instead.

The Cottinghams had not accepted her, but merely tolerated her. The stranger in the glade had come, not for love, but for murder. And now her imagined, kindly benefactor was the stranger who had kissed, then murdered. Had he brought her here, not for her protection, but to insure her conviction?

Her wits! Whatever had happened to them? "I. . .won't tell," she managed to say, and his progress toward her stopped. Turning, she almost lost her balance. She placed her hand to her mouth, lest she scream, and then ran for the door and wrenched it open.

"Jenny?" she heard him call, but she would not answer. The sound of his footsteps echoed in the hallway below her as she ran up the stairs, tripping several times on the steps.

After lifting her skirts and racing down the long hallway, she ran into her bedroom, slammed the door, and stood with her back against it. "I love him," she sobbed. "The man I love is a murderer. And he did it for me or my mother. His motives were noble. He could not bear for my mother to suffer any longer. He as much as admitted it."

Falling upon the bed, she grasped the covers in her hands and moaned into the comforters. She knew how she would pay for what he had given her. If his attorney could not prove her innocence, she would pay with her life.

seven

With a great shudder, Jenny rose from the bed. The near darkness enveloped her mind as well as the room. Lighting the candles, she reminded herself she had no one she could rely upon. Her mother was within the castle walls, but Nellie had informed Jenny that a doctor had been summoned to attend the grieving woman.

Jenny felt more alone than ever. She must find a course of action to take. And the first would be to rid herself of the notion that she was in love with that stranger who had kissed her in the glade. He was no longer a stranger, nor a fantasy, but a reality she had no idea how to deal with.

She barely responded when Nellie came in and offered to lay a fire. Jenny sat huddled in the big armchair with a comforter around her, as if she were freezing, staring at the ashes in the fireplace.

After the fire was glowing cozily, Nellie begged, "Oh, please, My Lady, you must let me have the duke summon a doctor for you."

"No, no. Not that," Jenny finally responded, much to Nellie's relief. "It's just that I've had so many surprises today, Nellie. Having my mother so near yet I still can't see her. . . . And the duke."

Nellie smiled, and her worried expression eased. Jenny then realized she must be careful not to let anyone suspect what she knew about Tilden. Putting her hand to her head she gave Nellie a sidelong glance. "I shouldn't confide like this, Nellie," she began. Nellie walked closer in eager anticipation. "But my encounter with the duke was so exhilarating and my gratitude for all he's done for me so overwhelming, well, I'm afraid it has all quite gone to my head."

Jenny thought that as good an excuse as any and would perhaps explain her actions, had anyone seen her run from the study to her room. Nellie seemed eager to accept her explanation and agreed that Jenny should rest.

The servant prepared the bed and fussed with the covers after Jenny climbed between the sheets. Jenny closed her eyes, pretending to sleep, but after Nellie tiptoed from the room, she opened her eyes and reviewed the events of the day.

It seemed an eternity ago that she had worried about being engaged to Ignatius Bodley. That concern paled when compared to the present situation. At least she had understood why her engagement had taken place. This situation baffled her.

What kind of man was Tilden Withington? Certainly he was no typical murderer. One couldn't call him deranged, for even Silas Bingham spoke of him with respect and knew him to be a fine and intelligent man. But why would he murder Bodley to save her from a loveless marriage and then let her take the blame?

She tried to recall everything Tilden had said to her. He, and even Mr. Bingham, had stated that Tilden's goal for many years had been to find her and force a confrontation with her mother. Before she knew Tilden Withington, she had thought him in love with her mother and suspected that he might step into his brother's place as her mother's husband. Perhaps she had been correct in that assumption, even though he was younger than her mother.

Then again, he might not have expected Jenny to be accused of the murder. And now he might think the courts would be more lenient with a young woman than with a man of his age.

But. . .she could not love a murderer, could she? Even if he did the horrible deed for her? Wasn't there some way to excuse it? Justify it? She shook her head in bewilderment.

What a terrible, terrible injustice she was doing him, if he were innocent. But if he hadn't committed the murder, who had?

That haunting question, first asked by Emmaline, brought her cousin to mind. Jenny didn't want her relatives to be guilty of the crime, but she must consider every possibility. Her life was at stake. The time of her trial grew closer. She would prefer the culprit be some irate father or intended of a young girl whom Bodley had wronged, but in her heart, Jenny knew nothing like that had arisen as a result of the magistrate's thorough questioning. The most likely candidate was someone much closer to her.

She shuddered. Uncle Thomas and Aunt Christine, particularly her aunt, were angry enough to have done it. But Emmaline, much as Jenny hated to admit it, was impulsive enough to have acted before giving the deed any thought. Perhaps in this setting, now that some time had passed, she and the Cottinghams could discuss the matter. Surely after having lived with them for eight years, she would be able to detect some kind of remorse or guilt on their faces.

Hastily, she went to the desk and scribbled a note to Bingham. *Am I allowed visitors? Could I see Sir Thomas, Lady Christine, and Emmaline?* After folding the note and sealing it, she summoned Nellie.

A short while later, Nellie brought Bingham's reply. *Lady Jenny. Your request will be presented to His Grace,* Bingham wrote. *You shall be informed of his response.*

Jenny realized anew how much control Tilden had over her life. A great shiver ran through her with the realization that even Bingham, whom she thought would be a confidante, was subject to the wishes of the duke.

She could not face Tilden again that evening and asked Nellie to convey her regrets and explain that she was exhausted and could not possibly dine in company.

A short while later, a knock sounded on her door. Would Tilden insist she come down for dinner? Would he accept no as her response? Jenny caught her breath when the door opened and the most beautiful woman she'd ever seen stepped inside.

"Jenny," the woman said and her voice broke. Then she managed to whisper, "I am. . .your mother."

Jenny rose and walked toward her. She could only stare at the trim lady of about her own height. The woman's black hair was sprinkled with gray and arranged in beautiful curls on top of her head. She wore no jewels around her neck. A single black curl trailed from the back of her head, around her lovely white neck, and onto the front of her soft blue gown, on which she wore a diamond broach. The blue of her dress matched the color of her eyes.

Forgetting all else, Jenny made the first move. "Mama," she breathed and took a step closer.

Her mother's eyes closed, and tears trickled down her pale cheeks. She swayed slightly. "Jenny," she said, her voice broken by a sob. "My baby."

Jenny rushed into her arms. "Oh, Mama. Is it really you?"

The woman could only moan, "My baby, my baby," over and over as she hugged Jenny, held her away and looked at her face, then drew her near again and touched her hair and her shoulders. "At last. At last. Oh, you don't hate me, do you, my darling?"

Jenny stepped back. "I could never hate you, Mama. I've always loved you. I couldn't remember what you looked like. No one would talk to me about you. But I often felt you were near. Nothing could make me happier than for you to be here. But. . .sit down. I was told you were ill."

She led her mother to a chair, then sat on the edge of her own chair, unable to take her eyes from the woman she'd thought was dead, but was here, facing her.

"Oh, ships make me so ill," her mother explained. "But I'm feeling much better now, and that dreadful headache is subsiding. I'm so sorry I couldn't see you the moment I arrived. But I could not let you see me feeling so miserably. I was afraid you might not want to see me at all."

Before Jenny could protest, her mother smiled through her tears. "But you, my darling. Nellie said you aren't feeling well."

"I'm much better now," Jenny assured her, reaching over for her hands. "Now that you are here."

Jenny's own face became moist with tears born of strong emotion. At least before she would be hanged, she had seen her mother.

"I will wait until you feel like eating," her mother said, dabbing at her eyes with a lace-trimmed handkerchief. "Then we shall dine together."

Wanting to spend time with her, Jenny's answer was forthright. "We can have dinner in my own dining area," she said, gesturing toward the room adjoining her bedroom. "I would be so happy if you would join me."

Over dinner, Jenny apologized to her mother. "I'm sure you would want to be with the duke in the dining room," she said reluctantly, wishing she did not have such an ache in her heart. Should she confide her suspicions to her mother, or even warn her that Tilden could be a murderer?

The older woman reached over and grasped Jenny's hand. "I only want to be with you, Jenny," she said sincerely. "Tilden understands this. He wants us both to be as happy as possible and looks for this unpleasantness to end."

Yes, Jenny thought. *But what happens when it's over? Will I have a life? Will I be imprisoned? Will I be hanged?*

"Do you want to tell me about it, Jenny?" her mother asked softly.

Jenny felt sure that this was partly what mothers were for—to listen to their daughters. What would happen if she told her mother of Tilden's presence in the arbor the night of Bodley's murder? Suppose Tilden denied it? Would her mother think her a liar? Or if she believed her, would her mother, who had already endured great suffering, find this unbearable?

After careful deliberation, Jenny shook her head. "I think it's enough that I tell Mr. Bingham." She picked at her food, then looked across at her mother's concerned face. Forcing herself to put thoughts of Tilden aside and concentrate on the wonder of having her mother with her, Jenny said, "I want to hear about you, Mama."

Jenny concentrated on her mother's story of sailing across the ocean to the New World and a new life. She didn't explain why she didn't take Jenny. She simply said the situation had become unbearable. "Without Stanford, I could not have endured the loss of you. Sometimes I think I must know how God felt to have given up His only Son. Nothing. . . nothing could be so distressing."

Jenny's questions remained unanswered as she watched the distress upon her mother's face and heard it in her voice.

"I counted my blessings. I had five wonderful years with you. My beautiful Jenny with the long black curls and huge blue eyes and loving arms." She blotted her tears again. "There was always a shadow on my happiness with Stanford. Then we came to understand the error of our ways. We had not known God when we ran away together, but once we came to understand His love for us, we experienced God's forgiveness." She reached over and grasped Jenny's hands. "I deeply regretted the pain my actions may have caused you and always prayed that God would watch over you."

Jenny looked down. Were the prayers not heard? She was accused of murder. She looked up to ask why she had been left behind. But her mother got a wistful look in her eyes. "I had sixteen years with Stanford, and our love never faltered," she said. "He gave me a wonderful life in America. He built me a gothic revival mansion on the Hudson River that was a model of one he sold in London."

Jenny smiled, glad that the conversation had turned more positive.

"His business ventures and intelligence made him a very influential man, constantly admonished to run for public office. He would not," she added, a look of regret crossing her face. "He feared the scandal would be uncovered and bring greater distress to me."

Scandal! That's what Aunt Christine had constantly alluded to. Jenny would not ask for details. She would accept whatever her mother wanted to tell her.

"We had a perfect life, with one exception," her mother continued. "That was my loss of you. After Stanford's death I thought you were lost to me forever. Now, Tilden has found you for me."

Jenny nodded. "I'm glad," she could say honestly, despite whatever had happened in the past. "Mama, I need you."

As they sipped their tea after dinner, a beautiful smile spread across the older woman's face. "My prayers that I might at least see you again have been answered," she said softly.

Jenny thought about those words. "Would your prayers help me, Mama?"

Her mother gazed down at her teacup for a long moment before answering. Finally she looked at Jenny and told her about her belief in God and how His Spirit had given her hope and strength. "Without God," she said earnestly, "I don't believe Stanford's and my love could have survived."

God helped love survive? "Does He always make things turn out right, Mama, if you pray?" Jenny asked wonderingly.

Her mother answered quietly. "Not in this life, Jenny. Not always. But sometimes our difficulties would be too much to bear without His presence."

"That sounds very nice, Mama, but I have so many things cluttering my mind." Jenny sighed. "Oh, but of course I believe in God," she added quickly, seeing the concern that the woman could not keep from her eyes.

"Even Tilden found that he needs God. He was very worldly as a young man, and he had everything this world considers important." Jenny's mother quickly named his extraordinary good looks, charm, wealth, intelligence, education, title, and place in royal circles. She talked of how Tilden had grown from a lad into a most responsible and respected man.

"He's very important to you, isn't he, Mama?"

A beautiful expression crossed the woman's face as she nodded and looked out beyond Jenny. "Next to Stanford, Tilden has been the most important person in my life, Jenny. You have always been in my heart and mind, darling," she assured hastily, "but I am speaking of those who were around me. Yes, I love Tilden with all my heart. One of the great joys of my life is that he has become a Christian."

So the two were in love, Jenny realized. Each had admitted it. Jenny's mother was not yet forty, and Tilden was in his early thirties. But a greater age difference lay between Jenny and Tilden. If only she had never kissed Tilden that night in the glade, things would be so much easier. She must forget. She must come to want Tilden and her mother to find happiness together. If only she could stop that silly heart of hers from longing for what could not be, from allowing unrealistic fantasies.

Suddenly, a new thought occurred to Jenny. "Mama," she said, moving to the edge of her chair. "You said Tilden is a Christian?"

"Yes, Darling."

"Christians could not commit murder, could they?"

Jenny's mother carefully considered her response. Her

daughter had asked a difficult question, and she had no idea why the young woman had raised such an issue. Her daughter knew so little about life and people, and no wonder, being whisked all over the country by her father, then becoming a part of the Cottingham household at a young age.

How could she tell Jenny that Christians could sin, that good persons could make terrible mistakes and commit dastardly deeds, without giving the impression that she condoned such actions? Could she tell Jenny that even murder could be forgiven? Or that all killings are not necessarily murder—but that some are acts of self-defense?

She set her cup down too close to the side of the saucer. It overturned. "Oh, I've made a mess," she said, exasperated.

"You're tired, Mama. We've talked for hours." Jenny went over to her mother and hugged her shoulders. "We've said it all tonight," she said. "Tomorrow there will be nothing to talk about."

The older woman laughed, grateful for the overturned cup. She'd rather blunder with tea than with the important issue Jenny had raised.

"Yes, I am tired, Jenny." She stood and put her hands on her daughter's shoulders. "Let's think on tonight's conversation and perhaps tomorrow we will talk and walk in the woods, or across the meadow, along the lake, or down by the sea. Our minds will be clearer."

Jenny nodded. They lovingly embraced, then parted for the evening.

For a long time, Jenny's mother sat in the first chair she came upon in her bedroom. She felt a chill deep into her bones. What had prompted that difficult, disturbing question Jenny had raised?

≈

The following morning, more questions developed in Jenny's mind.

"His Grace feels, and I concur," Bingham said, "that it would not be wise for the Cottinghams to visit."

"But they are my relatives," Jenny countered.

"True," Bingham agreed, "but as you yourself have told me, Lady Cottingham is not particularly fond of your mother. Even if your mother wished to receive her, Lady Cottingham might refuse. Tilden feels this would bring greater stress upon you both."

Jenny lowered her eyes to her hands. "I did not think of that."

"And too," Bingham added, "we do not wish to chance your saying anything that might disadvantage our case."

"Oh, but I wouldn't—"

"Not intentionally," Bingham replied. "But the slightest remark, or even silence, can tell another much about ourselves. Your face, my dear, is most expressive." He smiled in that fatherly way. "We do not want to chance anything hampering our chances for you, Jenny."

Jenny managed a trembling smile. Bingham kept referring to "we." Apparently, Tilden worked on the case too. He wouldn't want to do anything to upset Diane further—or to place suspicion on himself.

"Is there another suspect?" Jenny asked hopefully.

"As we have discussed, Jenny," Bingham reminded her, "we must have motive, opportunity, and evidence. There certainly are others who are more suspect than you, in my opinion," he added, with a contemplative expression in his eyes. "But I do not reveal too much, even to my clients, before we are in the courtroom."

"Do you talk over everything about the case with Duke Withington?"

"Everything that I feel is pertinent, Jenny."

Jenny looked away from his penetrating gaze. Did that mean Mr. Bingham was completely on her side in this—or did his primary obligation belong to Duke Tilden Withington, whose primary concern was his future with Lady Diane?

❧

Cool breezes blew across the meadow, where fragrant flowers had vanished, leaving behind a rich verdant green carpet of grass. Jenny knew that the cool English fog would soon be upon them, but for now she would enjoy the summer's warmth.

She and her mother rode through the forests and fields, then came upon a lake where they spread out the cloth for their picnic supper. They were laughing when Tilden rode up to them from the woods.

Jenny saw the delightfully startled look on her mother's face and detected the lilt in her voice when she exclaimed, "I feel like a child, doing this."

Tilden laughed too, equally joyful, then dismounted and tied his horse to a tree, several yards away. He returned to them and asked playfully, "What's this about a child?"

Jenny glanced at him and felt her cheeks grow suddenly hot. She quickly knelt and began to take items from the basket.

Her mother laughed again and held out her hands to him. "A child," she repeated. "I feel so wonderful."

Tilden laughed with her, holding her hands. "Ah, Diane. To hear the sound of your laughter again is music to my ears. And you look like a young girl. You two could be sisters."

"You flatterer," the older woman accused, then her voice softened. "Tilden. I'm so grateful to you. I never thought I would have reason to smile again. You have made it possible for me to have so much."

Jenny heard the warmth in his reply. "And I hope to give you even more."

"I know," her mother whispered. Jenny felt like an intruder. They must surely be speaking of marriage later on. The only thing which prevented it now was the upcoming trial.

Everything must wait for that.

"Join us, Tilden," Jenny's mother implored, her voice light and excited again.

A brief silence ensued before he replied. Jenny sensed they were looking at her. She held her breath lest he say he would join them.

"Another time, perhaps," he said. "I came to tell you that Bingham and I must go to London for several days. There is much to discuss with his partners."

Jenny still did not look up when he walked around and stood facing her. She could see his riding breeches and shiny black boots. Then he knelt in front of her. Looking around, she saw that her mother had gone to pick wild flowers near the edge of the wooded area.

"It's wonderful, Jenny," he said, "seeing you and Lady Diane like this."

Jenny could think of nothing to say, except, "Thank you." She glanced up quickly to find him staring at her intently. His eyes held an expression she felt should be reserved only for her mother after the things he had said to her. His smile was beautiful, and she could not keep from remembering how his lips had felt on hers that night in the glade. Quickly she looked down to his arms that rested upon his bent legs. His hands were almost near enough to touch her.

"No need to thank me, Jenny," he said with meaning. "I would do anything possible for you. Anything."

Even murder? Why? Because her mother had so desperately wanted to find her? Jenny found breathing difficult and put her hand to her slender neck. Her heart and mind were in such terrible conflict. Perhaps she should save them all a great deal of grief and simply ride the chestnut mare over the cliff and into the sea, rather than wait for the ordeal of a trial. That way, her mother and Tilden could find happiness together and Jenny would not have to fear blurting out the awful truth.

"Good-bye," she whispered.

Suddenly Tilden reached out and grasped her hand. Jenny closed her eyes against the feeling when he lifted her hand to his lips and she felt the gentle pressure of his kiss. Then he squeezed her hand gently. "Take care," he said, and she felt it sounded like a warning. He rose quickly and walked over to her mother.

Jenny watched as her mother put her arm through Tilden's and together they walked over to the duke's horse. Jenny turned her head and gazed out upon the water where fish dimpled the surface, making circles that appeared, expanded, then faded. That is what any personal thoughts of Tilden must do, she determined. Fade from her mind.

After Tilden mounted his horse and rode away, Diane walked over to the area where Jenny sat, apparently lost in thought. Diane sat gracefully at one edge of the cloth, beneath the shade of a tree, determined to enjoy this time with Jenny and share these invaluable moments.

"What were you like when you were young, Mama?" Jenny asked. "I would love to hear it all."

Looking into her past, Diane began talking about her early childhood that had been so happy. She had been the product of her parents' middle age, and their only child. Her father was Russian and her mother English. Their home life had been one of love and security.

Diane's parents had both Russian and English friends, as well as homes in both countries. At age fifteen, Diane had been informed by her parents that her marriage with Lord Greenough had been arranged. He and his first wife had visited their home many times when Diane was just a child. Later, in his widowed state, he had not visited as often. Diane had scarcely known him. Then, they were to be married.

"I don't mean to make your father out to be an ogre, Jenny,"

Diane said with difficulty. "He wasn't that at all. Nor were my parents unfeeling. They wanted the best for me and believed the marriage would provide that." Her voice grew sad. "I didn't know about love, Jenny. I had never loved any man except my father. William Greenough reminded me of him."

William was forty and Diane sixteen when they married. He was a polite, charming, handsome man with a title and wealth. But she had not understood her wedding night, after Lord Greenough had too much to drink. Diane had been terrified of him, but in his drunken state he had begun to insist upon his rights as a husband.

Later, she learned he had been devastated when he lost his first wife. He had taken to drinking and gambling. "If he had been more understanding of my innocence," Lady Diane said in defense of him, "or if I had known more about men, perhaps it would have been different. But that does not excuse what he did. Other men have faced disappointment without abusing their wives."

Because Diane feared him, he drank. When he drank, he became a forceful, violent figure who frightened her even further. But Diane determined to make the best of it. She learned to use her beauty and charm to induce him not to drink. She learned she could get her way by pretending to care for him more deeply than she did. But he always sensed her reluctance when he came near her.

A year passed. He drank more heavily and became insanely jealous. When they entertained or visited their friends, he proudly showed her off. She wore beautiful clothes and jewels, and he could not praise her enough. He caused all eyes to look at her. Then when they were alone he condemned her for the admiration she had received from the other men and accused her of seeking their attention.

Another year passed, and Jenny was born. Diane poured the love that she could not give to her husband on her child.

After she regained her figure, William proclaimed her more beautiful and desirable than before. Diane stopped trying to defend herself when he made his unfounded accusations. She simply turned her attention to her daughter. At that time, her parents were quietly living out their lives in their grand home in Russia.

Jenny was two years old when Diane met Duke Stanford Withington at a royal ball given at Withington Castle. The Greenoughs were announced, but before she could be personally introduced to the duke, she saw him from across the room. Later, when he asked her to dance, she politely told him she never danced with anyone but her husband.

He merely nodded, and she vowed she would never look at the man again, for strange, forbidden things were happening within her mind and heart. In spite of her resolve, during the course of the evening, her eyes continued to meet his.

That night, William Greenough struck her for the first time. His rage had been aroused when Stanford had asked her to dance. The fact that she refused made no difference. Diane said she would never go out in public again, but that did not please him. He wanted the world to know he had a young, beautiful wife.

On several occasions after that, she saw Stanford but refused to look at him. Then at one party, Lord Greenough was caught up at a gaming table, and Diane walked away from the other ladies. She stepped into the darkness and leaned against a tree. She had not wanted to think of seeing Stanford at the party for it caused only distress.

Suddenly he stood before her. He apologized for approaching her that first night, for since then he had heard of her husband's terrible jealousy. "I understand his feelings," he said, "for you are the most beautiful woman I have ever seen. And your actions prove you to be a wonderful lady. I will never approach you again."

Before she could speak, he turned to walk away. Just as he did, Lord Greenough appeared. Stanford attempted to dodge the blow, but Lord Greenough's fist made contact with his jaw. Stanford lost his balance and lay sprawled on the ground.

Then Lord Greenough's open hand whipped across Diane's face. Stanford jumped to his feet, but Diane feared for him more than for herself. "How dare you interfere," she said forcefully to Stanford, in an effort to reassure her husband of her loyalty. She caught Lord Greenough's arm and began walking with him toward the house. Even so, Lord Greenough began making ugly accusations that Diane knew Stanford could hear.

After they returned home that evening, William said he regretted Diane's undisciplined nature and was forced to teach her a lesson. He used a whip which made welts on her back, buttocks, and legs. After only a few lashes, he flung the whip away and began to sob, begging Diane's forgiveness. Diane cradled his head against her chest. He seemed like a sick child. He confessed that he had lost a huge sum of money at the gaming table and that loss had caused his violent outburst.

Diane forgave him. They both had been done a terrible injustice by the arranged marriage. The rising welts on her body did not hurt as much as the knowledge that her heart could never belong to her husband. They were past any form of reconciliation. It was then she asserted herself, telling him he must never again strike her or she would leave.

He apparently believed it, for he did not strike her again for a long time, but his accusations continued and he threatened that if she attempted to leave him, he would take Jenny from her. She became terrified.

On one occasion when Lord Greenough seemed not to be around, Stanford came near Diane again. "Can you not even speak to me?" he asked.

"No," she replied desperately.

"Then leave him," he implored. "I will take care of you. You must know."

"He will take my child if I even arouse his suspicions. Please go away."

Stanford did go away. But that did not stop Lord Greenough's jealousy. His gambling and drinking worsened. He lost most of both their fortunes.

During the year that Jenny turned three, Diane's parents died.

"You were four the night everything changed," Diane said. Lord Greenough had lost a huge sum and began making accusations again. They argued violently. He shouted that he was well aware that Duke Withington left any gathering the moment they arrived. Diane insisted that his actions proved that nothing was going on between them. Jenny awakened and began to cry. William Greenough yelled for her to be quiet, and when the frightened child continued to scream, he jerked her up and spanked her bottom.

Diane said nothing that night. For the next several weeks, Lord Greenough drank very little and gambled not at all. Diane knew he was making an effort to change, but it was too late.

When he had to be away for a few days, Diane visited a sympathetic friend who knew something of Diane's difficulties. Diane sent a note to Stanford, then met him in a wooded area near the friend's country home.

When Stanford arrived, Diane asked him if he would help her and Jenny get away from Lord Greenough. "Yes," he said, then took Diane in his arms and kissed her.

"He told me," Diane said to Jenny, while tears streamed down her face, "that we would not have a clandestine rendezvous and he would not kiss me again until I was free to love him as he loved me."

Jenny's heart ached for her mother.

"Oh, Jenny. I don't mean to imply that your father was a terrible man. He was a lonely, middle-aged man when he married me. I was too young and innocent for him. I can see these things upon looking back, but then, I wasn't mature enough to understand his nature and his problems. Then too, he could have chosen to act differently. Instead he did the very things that would cause what he feared most—that I might someday leave him."

"I know, Mama," Jenny assured her. "I loved my father. I knew much of his drinking was his way of numbing his pain. I felt sorry for him."

"I hope you weren't the target of his violent rages," her mother said. "That always worried me."

"He wasn't home much, Mama, and I learned not to go near him when he drank."

"If I had not fallen in love with Stanford, perhaps things would have been different. Maybe I could have established a separate household somehow to protect both you and me, but it didn't seem possible at the time because your father controlled all our money. And then I did fall in love. I didn't want to, but I couldn't help it. Later, both Stanford and I learned about God's love for us and repented of our sins."

"I don't blame you, Mama," Jenny said and looked down.

"I never knew a man could be so loving and yet so gentle with a kiss, until Stanford kissed me," Jenny's mother explained. "It was the kind of kiss that should have been my first one, not after so many years of marriage to another man."

Jenny reached over and held her mother's hands. She could understand. She knew that Tilden's kiss was exactly what a first kiss should be. But it should never have happened. Now she wondered if she had so reminded Tilden of her mother that he couldn't resist the kiss. He probably regretted it and hoped she would not tell her mother. And of course she wouldn't. No one else knew Tilden came to the glade that night. Now it was too late to tell anyone. Who would believe her if he denied it?

"Mama," she said quietly. "Could you love a murderer?"

Diane tried not to show her surprise at Jenny's unexpected question. Why would she ask it? But she mustn't avoid the question either. The best example she could think of was King David.

"You know about King David in the Bible, don't you, Jenny?" she asked.

"I've heard of him."

The words tugged at Diane's heart. Her dear child's education in the Scriptures had been sadly neglected. She gave a little background on the shepherd boy who became king.

"It all started when he gazed upon the beautiful Bathsheba from his rooftop, as she bathed," Diane said, trying to answer Jenny's question. "He did not turn away, as a gentleman should, but rather watched and desired her. Although he was a great and good man all of his life, he committed adultery with her. They fell in love, and King David caused Bathsheba's husband to be murdered so he could take her as his own wife." Diane concluded sadly, "He was punished and suffered for it."

She watched her daughter's troubled eyes. Her answer had caused Jenny pain. "But God forgave him," Diane hastened to add. "He can forgive. . .even murder."

"His wife," Jenny asked falteringly. "She lived with him after that? Did she love him?"

"From all indications," Diane admitted, "Bathsheba loved King David in spite of what he did."

Jenny's reaction indicated to Diane that her response had not satisfied her daughter. Diane shivered and realized the sun had disappeared from the sky and the air had grown cool.

"Darkness will be upon us soon," she said, beginning to gather the remains of the picnic. "Let's head back to the castle."

Jenny's sense of maturity and probing mind gave Diane reason to be careful in forming answers and advice for her daughter. She wasn't quite sure how to tell Jenny she had always loved her and always would. Yes! Even if she were a murderer.

eight

During the next several days, rain fell. Diane asked that a fire be laid in the drawing room where she and Jenny ate supper. After their dishes were removed, the two women remained, sipping tea and having their evening talks. The conversations remained light. Jenny did not ask the questions that lay heavy upon her heart. She did not want to believe that Tilden Withington would murder anyone. But if he had, her mother would still love him.

Then Tilden returned to the castle. Silas Bingham remained in London to work with his partners on the trial, which was fast approaching. During dinner, Jenny's mother and Tilden attempted to draw her into the conversation, to little avail. She dared not look at or speak to Tilden.

Then the two talked about something that had happened in America and referred to a previous conversation, of which Jenny had no part. But then, didn't people in love have their own private communication? She wasn't sure about anything anymore. During that moment in the glade, she had felt there was an understanding between herself and Tilden, one that went deeper than words.

Now, she knew that experience had been one-sided. She, only, had felt that special something that awakened her to love—that painful thing that tugged so at her heart. Obviously Tilden had not shared her feelings. He had already fallen in love with her mother.

"You've eaten so little, Jenny," she heard her mother say.

"Oh," Jenny said, looking up. She felt guilty meeting her mother's warm, tender expression. How would her mother feel if she knew Jenny had kissed Tilden?

Jenny was glad when they had finished dinner.

"Join Tilden and me in the library, Jenny," her mother invited. "We will have coffee or tea."

"I beg you to excuse me," Jenny said. "I've just finished reading a novel and would like to start another." Fearful that her mother would think she did not enjoy her company, she hastened to add, "The reading takes my mind off things."

"I understand, Darling," her mother replied, though obviously disappointed.

"What were you reading, Jenny?" Tilden asked.

"Moll Flanders," she replied. "I've never had so much time to read and think, and I suppose I'm overdoing it." She hoped she sounded convincing. It was true, but she would much rather spend a part of her evening with the two people she loved if the situation were different.

"Ah, but surely you can spare us a moment of your time, Jenny," Tilden said good-naturedly. He took her arm and led her away from the dining room and down the long hallway toward the library.

Tilden's eyes focused on Jenny, while he asked, "You have read the book, Diane?"

"Enjoyed it immensely," she replied with a light laugh. "What is it about human nature that enjoys such debauchery?"

"Debauchery?" Tilden asked. He arrived at the library door and held it open while the two ladies walked past him. He followed. "Defoe has stated quite clearly that his purpose was to point out the evil in it." His tone held mock-humor. "And you enjoyed it, Diane?"

Jenny's mother laughed. "A slip of the tongue on my part, Tilden," she said and winked at Jenny, who could not help but smile at her mother.

Jenny sat near the glowing, cozy fire that fought the coolness so common during late summer evenings. Tilden and her mother sat on a nearby couch.

"Fire feels good," Tilden said, and Jenny's mother agreed while pouring the coffee that a servant had brought in and set on the low table in front of the couch. Tilden leaned over to hand a cup to Jenny. "We'll turn you into a coffee-loving person yet," he quipped.

"I do like it," she responded, "but not as much as tea."

"Shall I get tea for you?" he asked.

"Oh, no," she replied quickly and looked over at him, then back at the cup for she felt a trembling in her hands when their eyes met. Would she forever be foolish like this? If she had known that one kiss with a stranger in a glade could be such a world-shattering event, she would never have done it. Never! Maybe with time, it would fade from her life. But it did not seem likely.

"We didn't get your opinion of the book, Jenny," her mother observed.

Jenny's mind had to work quickly to realize just what her mother referred to. After a sip of coffee she set the fine china cup in the saucer. "I liked it. And I think the heroine rather enjoyed her debauchery."

"Most of the characters did," her mother agreed. "Until they were caught in their crimes."

She cleared her throat, and to Jenny, the sound seemed nervous. Did her mother also believe that she had murdered Bodley? The cracking of the fire filled the silence.

ða

Tilden felt it important that Jenny talk—whatever the subject might be. But she didn't want to talk with him. What had he done to cause her to withdraw from him? At least they were in the same room, and she seemed receptive to a discussion about the book.

"Diane," he said, "do you feel genuine repentance occurred in the characters?"

Although Jenny did not look at them, he saw her chin lift slightly and knew she listened. It took all his willpower not to stare at her lovely profile aglow in the firelight. She seemed such a sweet, delicate creature, and he seriously wondered if a court of law could truly believe her capable of murder.

And yet, Jenny's young mother had been a beauty in both appearance and spirit, but the world had taken delight in condemning her, just as surely as if they had sentenced her to the gallows. Bingham often said that nothing could save Jenny from conviction except discovering who other than the girl had killed Bodley. With considerable effort, Tilden forced his attention back to Diane.

"For some of the characters," she said in response to Tilden's question, "their repentance became a last resort. One would have to see a change that took place in order to judge correctly."

"Wasn't Moll Flanders' repentance the reason she was deported rather than hanged?" Jenny asked.

A long moment passed before anyone spoke.

"Her semblance of repenting and talking with the minister and having him speak well of her surely played a part in it," Diane finally said in agreement.

"But her repentance apparently went no deeper than her words," Tilden added seriously. "Defoe, in his introduction, said there is no true repentance apart from divine intervention."

"I skipped the introduction," Jenny admitted, looking at him and seeming interested in his words.

Tilden smiled. "That's to be expected," he said. "However, Defoe is saying that one may wish to repent, even try, but sometimes be unable to do so."

"Are you saying that Moll Flanders was unable to repent?" Jenny asked, wide-eyed.

Tilden found his mind and emotions in terrible conflict and struggled to remind himself that he was not simply dealing with the young girl who had so desperately clung to him in that glade, whose lips had sought his, whose warmth he could feel close to him even while he reminded himself he was much too mature and sensible for such thoughts.

Unable to look upon her any longer, he set the near-full cup of coffee on the table, stood, and walked over to the fireplace, where he propped a foot on the hearth. How he would like to take Jenny by the shoulders and shake her until she revealed what lay in her heart and in her mind. He longed to know, but she kept herself far removed from him. He had to stand and pretend interest in a discussion of that book.

"It seems to me," Tilden managed to say in a normal tone after a much-needed deep breath, "that she used anything and anyone—whatever seemed advantageous at the moment."

"Would not anyone do the same when fighting for his life?" Jenny asked in a small voice, her eyes fastened on the cup she held.

In carefully chosen words, Tilden replied, "The instinct for survival is that strong. Yes."

Diane's voice sounded unnatural. "But Tilden and I have heard so many sermons on repentance, Jenny. You have not had the opportunity, have you, Dear?"

Jenny shook her head.

"We will have to correct that," Tilden said suddenly, removing his foot from the hearth and facing Jenny. "Sunday we will have the minister come and deliver his sermon on 'Repentance.' And afterward, if we wish, we shall discuss Defoe's book with him."

He deliberately lowered his voice an octave and spoke with mock gravity. "For teaching purposes only. The minister would not enjoy the debauchery."

When Jenny laughed with him and Diane, Tilden felt exultation flow through his veins. Her laughing eyes met his before she lowered them to her cup. He wanted more of these discussions, but on less morbid subjects. He walked over to a shelf, took a book from it, and returned to Jenny.

"Have you read this one?" he asked.

Jenny carefully put the cup and saucer on the table, then glanced at her mother. Tilden noticed a questioning look in Diane's eyes that was quickly replaced by the warm expression she always had when looking at Jenny. Although a servant would have done it at a moment's notice, Diane began to stack the cups and saucers onto the tray.

Jenny stood to take the book from him. *"Emma,"* she said with a sense of awe. "No, I haven't read it. But I have often heard it spoken of. Aunt Christine and Uncle Thomas's friends have discussed it, but of course I wasn't allowed to enter the discussion. I must confess, I often listened to conversations outside closed doors."

"Oh, Jenny," Diane said, her voice choked. "You always had such an inquisitive mind, a quick mind, even when you were little. If only you could have been with me and Stanford. You should never have had to seek information from behind closed doors."

Jenny stared at the book cover, looking uncomfortable. "Mama," she said softly. "Mama, these past days with you have been wonderful. I'm glad that I can talk to you, and be near you, and love you. It really has been the happiest. . ." Her voice trailed off as she turned to look at her mother's tear-streaked face.

"I know," Diane said in a whisper, walking near. "I know what it's like to be happy and yet so desperately miserable."

Jenny nodded and, grasping the book tighter in her hands, turned from both Tilden and her mother and ran out the door.

"I'm sorry," Jenny heard her mother say, but she had not moved quickly enough, for out of the corner of her eye she saw her mother turn toward Tilden with a cry upon her lips, and then Tilden's arms reached out and enveloped her.

Jenny ran up the steps and into her bedroom. She wished she could pour out her fears and longings to her mother. They had wonderful conversations about so many things, but never about Jenny's innocence or guilt. Diane often said that Jenny was brave, but Jenny knew it wasn't bravery on her part. It was fear. Fear that if she talked about it to her mother, then she would have to express her doubts about Tilden.

Jenny did not know how to tell her mother that she suspected Tilden was a murderer. Perhaps her mother already knew. But that would not stop her from loving Tilden. Even such a thing as that did not always destroy love. She knew. Yes, she knew, for her mother had said Bathsheba loved David even after she knew he had murdered her own husband. And Jenny knew she would always love her mother—no matter what. Besides, if she talked about that night, she would have to confess that Tilden had been in the glade with her. She must remain silent.

Forcing herself to begin reading *Emma* after slowly moving her fingers over the cover where Tilden had touched it, Jenny soon realized she was beginning to read a story about a girl who would most likely fall hopelessly in love. Had that been Tilden's intent when giving her the book? Perhaps to impress upon her the hopelessness of anything? He had made it possible for these past weeks to be both her happiest and, as her mother had said, "most miserable."

nine

Rain fell all day Sunday, but the lighted candles lent a cozy glow to the little chapel. A warm fire sent dancing lights along the shadowed stone walls. Diane sat on the wooden bench between Jenny and Tilden. Several of the servants attended, as did Tilden's valet and secretary. Nellie, her mother, and Mrs. Millet occupied the back row.

The minister, a small man with thinning hair that was streaked with gray, had piercing dark eyes under bushy eyebrows. Jenny had thought he could do with the eyebrows on his head and smiled at the thought. His pale skin caused Jenny to wonder if he were ill, but after he began to speak, his face took on color, his eyes glowed, and his voice reflected the seriousness of his message.

She felt uncomfortable when he quoted, "All have sinned, and come short of the glory of God," however her spirits lifted when he said Jesus came and died to save mankind from their sins, to forgive, and give them eternal life.

Jenny liked the sermon, feeling it adequately defined repentance, clarifying some of the points about the novel that she, Tilden, and her mother had discussed. She felt particularly comforted when the minister quoted a wonderful verse: "Come unto me, all ye who are weary and heavy laden, and I will give you rest."

She did not take her eyes from the minister but became so engrossed in his words that she even forgot her first impression of him as a rather homely man. Jenny knew he spoke primarily for her benefit, for he seldom glanced at the others. She only regretted that she must sit and listen, rather than comment and ask questions about his fascinating, intelligent, and emotionally moving dissertation.

Then, as if sensing her undivided attention and reveling in it, he spoke of God's willingness to forgive even the most heinous of crimes, adding that one must believe in Jesus as the Son of God and invite the Spirit of that living Jesus into one's heart.

She began to wonder just why Tilden had invited the minister. Was it to convince her that he had been forgiven, even though she would have to pay for his crime? Was it so Jenny could pretend to receive forgiveness so she might be deported rather than hanged? Would his conscience be free if she were allowed to live? Her thoughts went round and round, and suddenly she realized her hands were pressed against her cheeks.

Then she heard the minister's voice near her ear. He stood in front of her. "Would you like to accept this living Jesus into your life?" he asked.

Jenny looked at him in horror. He believed she was guilty! The chapel no longer seemed warm and cozy. It had become a place where she was expected to confess to a crime she had never committed and find forgiveness.

If she said she would like to accept this forgiveness, wouldn't it be like admitting murder to a room full of witnesses? Wouldn't it simply further insure her being found guilty? How could Tilden do such a thing?

But wouldn't a murderer do anything? Didn't he say that one would do almost anything when it came to survival?

A cry escaped her lips as she ran past them all and tore out of the chapel. Finding a door, she flung it open and rushed out into the torrential rain, her shoes becoming soaked from the muddy streams rushing over the courtyard. Within seconds, her clothes clung to her body like skin, and the icy lash of the deluge stung her face like whips, as if nature itself forbade any escape.

Having never before come into the courtyard from the direction of the lower floor, Jenny looked around helplessly. By that time, Nellie grasped one of her arms and Mrs. Millet the other.

"Let her go," a stern voice commanded. Then Tilden addressed her from the doorway. "Come inside before you catch your death of cold."

Jenny felt the hands release her arms. Released, also, was the possibility of her rushing down to the sea and flinging herself from a cliff. No one would allow her the luxury of hastening her inevitable fate. Mrs. Millet, seemingly unobtrusive, always stood nearby, on guard.

Then Jenny remembered Bingham saying that the servants would prevent her leaving. And whatever had happened to her wits? Or her courage? Or her gratitude not to have been incarcerated in a prison? Or concern for her mother's feelings?

Her mother stood just inside the doorway, her face a mask of concern. The minister stood behind her. Tilden stepped out into the rain, and Jenny could not bear his coming to force her inside. She must do that on her own. She had nowhere else to go anyway. Nowhere!

Bravely she lifted her chin, welcoming the cold pelting rain that served as a slap upon her face, reawakening her realization that she must not allow such impulsive emotions to overtake her. "I'm sorry," she said, looking toward the drenched Nellie and Mrs. Millet, standing on either side of her.

"Let me help you change and get you warm," Nellie pled.

Jenny nodded, then felt the comforting hand on her arm.

"I'll be all right," Jenny said and began to walk toward the doorway. She did not look at Tilden, standing in the rain.

But his hand shot out and grasped her arm. "Leave us," he said to the others.

"No," Jenny exclaimed, more terrified now than she had been at the minister's words. Looking around, she saw the uncertainty on each of their faces, but they had to obey the duke. His word was law. They quickly retreated into the castle.

"I'm. . .wet," Jenny stammered, looking down at the clothes plastered to her skin. She trembled, not only because she felt cold, but because of the nearness of Tilden.

"So am I," he replied. "But that can be remedied. Now tell me, where were you going, Jenny?" he asked, his face a strange mask. She felt herself shaking uncontrollably.

"To. . .to the sea," she gasped. "Let me end it now. I can't bear this waiting any longer. I can't." She tried to sidetrack him but succeeded only in turning far enough to feel the stone walls behind her. There was no escape, for Tilden restricted her retreat from the front.

Her breath caught in her throat, and she had to part her lips to take in enough air. His arm came up, and she felt the wetness of his coat sleeve where it pressed against her own bare flesh above the drape of her soggy gown. She became quite unaware of the cold, for his hand cradled the back of her neck. Her eyes closed against the bending of his head toward her. Momentarily everything was forgotten in her great desire to be lost in his arms.

As if with a will of their own, her arms came up to embrace him. She felt the press of his sleeve against her soft flesh and the sweet roughness of his face against her cheek, the feel of his breath, hot against her ear. She felt as if she were drowning as surely as if she had plunged from the cliff. A delicious fear traveled throughout her body, rising as a wave that grew higher and higher.

"I cannot let you go, Jenny," he said, his voice raspy with emotion. "I will have you watched more closely to prevent your doing something drastic. We cannot lose you. I cannot."

The difficulty with which he spoke the words and the desperation in his voice reached her, dispelling the warmth and plunging her into icy depths.

Her arms fell to her sides. Realization swirled around her like the cruel wind. Cold and hard, the stone wall dug into her back. Wet and cold, his sleeve now chilled her body.

How could she have imagined his hand on her neck could be a caress? Was it not, instead, a grasp that could easily choke the life from her? Were not his words both a threat and a warning? And worse, was she not totally deranged for wanting to be in the arms of such a man?

What were Nellie's words? The women were wild for the Withington dukes. But the men of the family had that blood-thirsty, adventurous streak in them. Tilden wasn't in battle for a king. But the same loyalty and devotion he felt toward her mother would cause Tilden to see this situation through to the end—no matter what. Even if it meant taking the life of Ignatius Bodley—and allowing Jennifer Greenough to be hanged.

"Please, I. . ."

Sensing her helplessness, Tilden moved away from her. He had hoped to quell her desire to fling herself into the sea, to impress upon her that such a move would be folly, and bring acceptance to her mind. He apparently had failed in his efforts, however, for now she seemed like a caged animal, fearful and longing to retreat from its captor.

He regretted the words he had felt compelled to say to her, but he must give instructions for her to be guarded more carefully lest she harm herself. Watching her creep along the stone wall, inching away from him, holding onto the wall for support, he recalled his first sight of her from the top of the staircase. *I have found her,* he had thought. He had been unable to take his eyes from her but had watched her every move. Her beauty had captivated him. He would have known her anywhere, for she was a younger version of the lovely Diane. If only he could tell her how he truly felt. But for now, he let her disappear up a flight of stone steps.

Suddenly Tilden became aware of his wet clothing and shivered in the cold. If only the trial were over. Then he could speak his mind freely. Bingham had reported that he had very strong suspicions about the murder of Bodley and that it could be linked to another murder. The lawyer would say no more, but Tilden knew it would be a grave error in the eyes of all concerned if another tragedy occurred, such as Jenny's untimely death. Yes, he would increase his servants' watch on her.

🙠

Jenny fled to her bedroom and locked the door. As she reviewed the tumultuous events of the day, she had no choice but to accept the fact that she would not be allowed to take her own life. No, her fate was a dishonorable death by a hangman's noose. The closer the approaching trial came, the more she realized how slim her chances of acquittal. Hadn't her guilt already been decided when the official accusation had been made against her? Wasn't Bingham chasing a phantom stranger, supposed to have been in the glade that night?

If Bingham discovered the identity of that stranger, would he believe that Jenny's benefactor was trying to send her to the gallows rather than save her from them? Of course not! The idea was preposterous, even to herself. And Duke Tilden Withington would be quite aware of his power over Bingham.

If only she could talk with someone about it. But there was no one, not even her mother.

Much later a servant brought her dinner.

"Do you mind if I join you?" Jenny's mother asked, stepping inside the room.

Jenny shook her head but resolved not to discuss the chapel incident. The two women ate in silence for awhile, then engaged in safe and guarded chatter.

Suddenly the conversation took an unexpected turn. "Jenny," said her mother, "I must make you believe that neither Tilden nor I expected the minister to speak directly to you, and we are sorry."

Jenny looked at her mother's distressed face, not knowing what to say. "To repent, Mama," she asked, "would have done what? Would it have gotten me deported? Or would it make me appear guilty? Shouldn't I wait until after I'm convicted?"

"Oh, Jenny!" Her mother gasped and stood. "We had no thought of such a thing." She spread her hands helplessly. "We were only concerned about your eternal soul. We would have done the same if there were no charge lodged against you. Oh, please, believe me."

Jenny stood and allowed her mother to embrace her. She reveled in having her mother's arms around her. Suddenly she realized she could tell her mother anything without risking losing her love. But she would not tell her mother anything that might cause her more pain than she had already experienced. She knew her mother was happy to be with her, but always miserable because of the threat that hung over them. It must have been that way when she was married to Stanford—happy, yet miserable.

"Mama," she said finally, moving back and taking her handkerchief to wipe away the tears that streaked her cheeks. "I wonder if maybe I could go into the city."

"Into the city? Darling, you know you can't leave here."

Jenny stepped back and began to slowly pace the floor. "Yes, I know. But I thought it might be possible for me to see Bingham. I need to talk to him."

"Well, we can send for him," her mother said confidently. "He would come immediately."

"I know," Jenny said, realizing her mother would not understand. She could not confess to her mother the unbearable prospect of facing Tilden again. His presence completely disoriented her and made her inadequate to cope with the issues that Bingham had said she must try to be clear-headed about. "I feel a need to talk to him. I mean, away from here. I have imposed upon Duke Withington enough already."

"Imposed? Whatever do you mean, Child?"

"Well," Jenny tried to explain, gesturing helplessly. She had never been good at lying. She was simply trying to find a way to escape the castle, Tilden, and the accusations that seemed to weigh heavily upon her. But such an explanation would never be understood. "I have accepted Duke Withington's generosity and am unable to reciprocate graciously. I really don't like being beholden."

Her mother sank slowly into the nearest chair. "What do you mean, his generosity?"

"Well, Mama," Jenny said. "Everything! His house. His servants. His money bought the dress I'm wearing. Even the food I eat—"

"You don't know?" her mother interrupted.

"Know what, Mama?"

"Bingham didn't tell you? I assumed during all those weeks before Tilden and I came, he would have told you."

"Told me what, Mama?"

"Sit down, Jenny," she said. Jenny obediently sat in a chair across from her.

"As you must know, Jenny, Stanford was a very wealthy man. I shall never want for anything that money can buy. He left the controlling interest of the businesses in America to Tilden. But Stanford always considered you his child, because you were mine.

"Of course he knew better," she added quickly. "But he loved you because you were mine. Jenny, this castle is half mine. The other half belongs equally to you and Tilden. Stanford also left a considerable sum of money that only you can touch."

Jenny stared at her mother, trying to comprehend her words.

"Jenny," she assured, "you have taken nothing from Tilden financially. Oh, he might pay for items from his own money, but you could easily repay him. You are a very wealthy woman."

The news was quite shocking. But with the realization of her wealth, an unwanted thought pierced her heart with the force of a dagger.

She must try to remain calm. Plan something. She would send a servant for Bingham. Or perhaps she would ask a servant to ready a carriage to take her into London. Perhaps Nellie. But Tilden had increased the guard on her. That wouldn't work.

"This does put a new light on things," Jenny said carefully. Then she rubbed her temples. "But Mama, I am afraid the emotional events of this day have left me with a frightful headache. Would you mind if I lay down and rested for a bit?"

"Not at all," her mother said, concern in her eyes. "I'll send Nellie right away with some cool cloths." After giving Jenny a gentle kiss on her brow, she left the suite.

Jenny allowed Nellie's faithful ministrations, then listened to the wind howling against her windows, as if to warn her that even nature was set against her. Somehow she had to talk to Bingham and tell him of her suspicions. Shivering beneath the covers, she waited until near dawn. The rain had stopped and the wind had abated. Looking down onto the courtyard far below, her heart seemed to stop, for something moved. Then she breathed more easily. It was only a shadow made by a sudden gust of wind through the branches of the trees, or else it had been a reflection of the moonlight peeping through the clouds that raced across the sky.

If she could reach the chestnut mare, she could make it. No one would expect her to try anything so soon after Tilden's warning against an escape attempt. There were no windows in the dressing room, so no one would see the glow from the single candle she lit. Hurriedly dressing in her riding habit, Jenny felt mounting excitement stirring within. This was the sort of thing she should have done instead of attending Bodley's engagement party. How differently everything would have turned out.

Or would it? Duke Tilden Withington would have found her, somewhere, anywhere, regardless of what she had done, for he had been so determined. She would have remained unsuspecting. At least, now she knew of the danger.

Holding her breath, she crept along the silent, cold stone walls until finally reaching the courtyard. Safety! Almost! If she could get to the distant tree. Oh! That wasn't a tree. The shadow she had seen from the window was indeed a person. Tilden. Her heart sunk into her stomach. Failure. Failure again!

Tilden called her name and held out his hands toward her. He moved forward.

Helplessness, like a shadow, stole over her. For the second time in her life, she felt a welcomed darkness begin to descend upon her. Before she completely lost consciousness, his strong arms came around her, lifting her. As her cheek touched his shoulder, she had but one thought. *I am in the arms of my beloved enemy.* Then there was only darkness.

ten

Two days later Silas Bingham arrived. Tilden had sent a servant to London to summon the lawyer after Jenny had explained her reason for being in the courtyard the morning she had encountered Tilden.

"Couldn't you tell me you wished to see him?" Tilden had asked. Jenny had not answered, afraid to admit that she couldn't trust him.

Silas Bingham had a way of calming her, assuring her that the real murderer would be apprehended.

"Do you mean," she asked fearfully, "that you have discovered the whereabouts of the stranger in the glade with me that night?"

Bingham focused his stern eyes on her for so long, she had to escape his gaze by looking down at her hands. She took his silence for denial that the stranger had been found. And of course, she knew he could not have been, unless they had apprehended some innocent person.

It was the time to tell Bingham, to disclose all she had suspected and to expose Tilden. But as she tried to speak the words, they stuck in her throat. What would her life be like if she condemned the man she loved? How could she send Tilden to the gallows? How could she and her mother ever have a loving relationship if Jenny were the cause of Tilden's arrest? Her mother would certainly understand, but the gulf would be there, just the same.

Jenny looked across at Mr. Bingham, who patiently observed her, waiting for whatever she might disclose. Her lips trembled as she slowly shook her head. The words would not come. She could not accuse Tilden of murder.

"I'm sorry, Mr. Bingham. What seemed so urgent was only a foolish notion. There is nothing more I can tell you. Please forgive me for taking you away from your responsibilities in London. All we can do at this point is hope for the best."

No amount of persuasion on Bingham's part could induce her to reveal what lay at the base of her fears and frustrations. "Do you have any other suspects?" she asked, with only a minute hope that she was wrong in what seemed daily to become more and more a reality.

"None, Jenny, other than those I've had all along. And suspicions are not enough. In court, Jenny, we must have more than even certainty. We must present motive, opportunity, and evidence, either literal or circumstantial."

Jenny felt as if a weight were pressing on her chest. She could see how a prosecuting attorney would present her motive and opportunity, along with the evidence of arsenic in a glass. No matter what she might say, she could see the accusing finger pointing nowhere else but at her.

❧

"What did she say?" Tilden asked Bingham anxiously after Jenny left the study and went riding.

"Very little," the lawyer replied, wearing a worried look. "What happened while I was away, Tilden?"

Tilden shook his head. "Lady Diane told her of the inheritance, and the news had a strange effect on Jenny. She attempted to run away. Then she was so frightened, she fainted. Perhaps I am imagining things," Tilden added, "but I think she has withdrawn from me since the first day her mother and I arrived from America. Something I said, or did, has alienated her from me."

"Can you supply a reason, Tilden?" Bingham asked, his voice heavy with accusation.

Tilden turned toward the window where he could look out

at the trees, golden, brown, and red in the warm afternoon sunshine. The rain had stopped yesterday. It would be wonderful to ride about the grounds with Jenny and to watch her long black hair bounce in the wind and see the golden glow the warm sun would bring to her face. There was so much he would like to do.

"I suppose it's natural for her to be afraid, and more so as the time for the trial draws nearer," Tilden said finally.

"But she remained optimistic before you and Lady Diane arrived, Tilden. Something has changed."

Tilden turned toward Bingham, knowing the man would be honest. "You believe in her innocence, don't you?"

The attorney remained silent.

"Bingham!" Tilden almost shouted, staring fiercely at the man.

Bingham stood and lightly tapped the side of his cheek with his finger. "Has it occurred to you, Tilden," he asked, pointing that finger at Tilden, "that Jenny might have a mental lapse about that night?"

Tilden swallowed hard and shook his head. "It's impossible that she—"

"No, not impossible," Bingham interrupted. "She knows something she is not telling. Something that has bothered her since you and Lady Diane arrived."

Tilden stared at Bingham. "I don't understand."

"Neither do I," Bingham replied. "But I intend to. After dinner tonight, we'll talk. You and I and Jenny. Here in the study."

"How do you propose to get her here with me?" Tilden asked skeptically. "She avoids me now."

"I shall demand it," Bingham replied. "And you will accuse her of murder."

"What?" Tilden stormed. "Have you gone mad?"

"It must be done. That is exactly what will happen in the courtroom."

"Bingham, don't you know how devastating that will be for Jenny? To think that everyone, including me, believes she murdered Bodley?"

"It must be done, Tilden. Her mother cannot, so it must be you who accuses her. We must shock her into disclosing whatever she has shut up in her mind—these things that frighten and confuse her."

Tilden opened his mouth to protest, but he saw the wisdom of Bingham's words and intentions. He turned to face the window again.

"You must!" Bingham repeated.

❧

Jenny felt braver with Bingham in the castle and consented to eat dinner in the formal dining room. The conversation remained light and centered on happenings in the city. With summer nearing an end, the weather became a topic, and Jenny's mother noted how the leaves were changing so quickly even on the cliffs near the sea.

For the present, Jenny did not fear for her life. All Tilden had to do was wait, and the court would handle the rest.

After dinner, Jenny asked Bingham to linger in the dining room for a moment. The others left them in privacy. "I wish to leave the castle," she asserted. "Even if I am to be placed in a prison while awaiting trial."

Bingham sighed heavily and looked down at the toes of his shoes. "Let's discuss it in the library, Jennifer." He took her by the arm and led her into the hallway where her mother and Tilden waited.

"Come with us, Mama," Jenny said when they neared the study.

"I don't believe Mr. Bingham wants me there, Darling," she replied.

The lawyer did not contradict her, so Jenny nodded and followed him into the library. To her shock, Tilden followed and stood with his back against the closed door, blocking any escape.

"I thought we would be alone," she said, turning toward Bingham, her discomfiture obvious.

"The three of us should discuss this." Bingham held out his hand, indicating that Jenny should sit in the chair near the fireplace.

She sat, wondering if Bingham realized that Tilden was involved. Surely a famous attorney with his reputation would know such things. But perhaps Bingham saw Tilden simply as his client. After all, hadn't Tilden approached him about taking this case? Wouldn't Bingham's primary obligation be to the duke rather than to her?

Tilden sat on the couch across from her. Bingham took a chair at the side of the fireplace, in the shadows. It seemed to Jenny that only she and Tilden were in the room, making her uncomfortable. She sank back against the chair.

Bingham outlined the case, making it clear that their only defense was lack of motive on Jenny's part. She had everything to gain by Bodley's staying alive.

"I had nothing to gain," Jenny protested.

"Ah, but by the standards of society, Jenny, you had everything to gain married to a man who could give you all the world's goods and escort you into royal circles."

"I'd rather. . ." She hesitated, then added, "Die."

"How did you do it, Jenny?" Tilden asked suddenly. "How did you manage to sneak the arsenic into the glass without Bodley or someone else knowing?"

Hearing her gasp and seeing the devastation shrouding her face, Tilden stood and walked over to the fire, his back to Jenny. He shot a murderous glare at Bingham. How could this possibly do anything for Jenny? He'd only hurt her further.

Glancing back at Jenny, he saw the horror in her eyes. Misery rested upon her countenance as she lowered her eyes to her lap. Her chin began to tremble.

Tilden could bear it no longer. With a fierce glare at Bingham, he turned and strode over to Jenny, knelt in front of her, and took her cold fingers in his hands.

"Forgive me, Jenny. I know you didn't kill Bodley. I've never believed that. Please say you forgive me?"

She would not look up or speak. "If I had stayed that night, Jenny," he said low, "perhaps you would not be on trial. But I was in such a state over having found you. Years of searching had been futile. Then, there you were, a beautiful picture. I wondered if you were a figment of my imagination."

Jenny did not understand. He had just accused her of murdering Bodley, yet now he admitted in front of Bingham that he'd been there that night. She shook her head in confusion. "If you had stayed, then we both might have been accused of murder," she said with some difficulty.

She felt his hands stiffen against hers but knew she could not back down now. "Or," she said almost under her breath, "it might have been you who was implicated and not me at all."

"I don't understand, Jenny. Please explain." His voice held authority, and she feared looking into his eyes. She pulled her hands away, and he stood.

"All right," she said with a sense of determination. "I cannot keep this to myself any longer. You told me not to mention that you were there."

"But that was before the murder, Jenny. When I said that, I didn't know the murder was going to take place."

Jenny wanted desperately to believe that, but the evidence she had kept to herself was overwhelming. And if a person would murder, there was nothing to stop him from also telling a lie.

"It might have been your glass that had the poison in it," she protested.

Tilden stooped down again and took her by the shoulders,

shaking her gently. "What are you saying, Jenny?"

A sob escaped her throat. She felt his hands pressing into her shoulders but could hold back no longer. He became more insistent and shook her harder. "What do you mean, my glass?"

"The one you brought to the glade and set on the table," she said accusingly.

Tilden made a noise much like a snort. "I forgot that I took a drink to the glade. I didn't want it, but I hadn't wanted to make myself conspicuous by refusing."

Jenny recalled that Bingham had said many times something seemingly insignificant always tripped up the criminals. Is this what would trip up Tilden?

"That night," Tilden said emphatically, "there were much more important things on my mind, Jenny, than a drink. When I think of it, and I assure you I do quite often, it is not a drink I remember."

Jenny could not stop the sudden emotion that flooded her being. Warmth flooded her face, and she knew Tilden would notice.

"So you think I killed Bodley," he said in a tone that frightened her.

"I didn't want to think it. But what else could I think? A stranger. One who kissed me and held me the first time he saw me. Then. . .then. . .telling me to say nothing. What else could I think? I knew it was in the newspapers, and I felt if the stranger were innocent, he would come to my rescue. I even dreamed he would." Unable to hold in her doubts any longer, she continued. "I wondered why he did not come and proclaim me innocent. Then. . ." She hesitated and would not meet his eyes. "I realized he could not."

"Why could he not?" Tilden asked.

"Because instead of proving me innocent, he might be letting himself in for arrest as an accomplice, or. . ."

"Or?" he asked, urging her on.

Her voice became a whisper. "Or he might even be suspected of murder."

Tilden let go of her shoulders, stepped back, and almost lost his balance. "You honestly think I killed Bodley?"

She drew in her breath. She knew it was dangerous to tell a murderer that she knew what he had done, but she could not hide the secret any longer. "I no longer think you tried to kill Lord Bodley."

Just as a sigh of relief escaped his throat and a light gleamed in his eye, she lifted her chin courageously and looked past him, toward the fire. After a moment of hesitation, she continued. "I think. . .that you might have been trying to kill me."

"What?" he shouted fiercely.

Jenny looked up into his glaring eyes and covered her mouth with her hand to stifle a scream.

"Why would I want to kill you?" he demanded.

Tears formed in her eyes. He waited, then asked in a calmer tone, "Could you tell me how I attempted to. . .murder you?"

"The drink," she said.

"The drink?"

"Yes," she replied. "The drink you set on the table. If you wanted to murder me, then you would expect or hope that I might drink it after you left."

"How can you be sure he drank from my glass?" Tilden asked.

"I have pictured it over and over and over," Jenny replied. "Lord Bodley came into the glade, weaving back and forth and holding a goblet. I remember distinctly that he drained it and set the empty glass on the table. Then awhile passed as he came at me, and I pushed him away. He made crude remarks, then sat at the table and talked about our wedding day when I would behave more favorably toward him. He picked up your glass and began to drink from it. Not long after that, he died."

No one spoke. Jenny felt she must continue. "So, perhaps the poison was not intended for Bodley after all. Perhaps it was intended for me."

With a cry, Bingham jumped to his feet. Jenny had forgotten he was there, but now he and Tilden faced each other. An expression of shock rested on both their faces.

"This is a development I had not anticipated," Bingham remarked in a disgusted tone. "If I am indeed the best lawyer in Europe, then God pity the poor souls at the mercy of lesser attorneys." He shook his head dejectedly.

"And why, Lady Jennifer," he asked pointedly, "why would Duke Tilden Withington wish to murder you? Would it not make more sense for the culprit to be someone in the Cottingham family? Were they not all terribly distraught when Bodley sought your hand in marriage, rather than Lady Emmaline's?"

"They certainly perceived that as an insult," Jenny said. "But what the Cottinghams wanted most was Bodley's money and access to royal circles. They were quite angry at the onset; however, that anger abated and they accepted, even wanted, my marriage to Bodley after being convinced he would not marry Emmaline. My death, or Bodley's, would be the last thing any of them would want."

"Motive, motive," Bingham almost shouted. "Why would Duke Withington want your death?"

Tilden had walked to the other side of the fireplace. She felt slightly braver with Bingham between them. "For two reasons," she replied. "One, because he did not wish to share the inheritance that his brother left to both of us. After all, I am an outsider, not blood-related to my mother's late husband. Another reason is because. . ."

When she hesitated, Bingham stepped closer. "Because?"

"Because I would just be in the way. He is in love with my

mother. He found me for her. That endears him to her. But now, I am a nuisance with whom his money, and her attentions, must be shared."

"Very good motives," Bingham said finally.

Jenny tried to keep the tears from leaking out, but soon they moved unchecked down her cheeks. A small hiccup escaped her throat. She returned to her chair, lest she fall.

Tilden took out a clean folded handkerchief from his inner pocket and knelt beside her. Gently, he wiped her tears.

"Jenny," he whispered and she looked at him. She could not bear the beautiful smile on his lips or the warmth in his eyes. He should not look at her that way, but he was a rake who had plotted her death.

He lifted her hand and touched it with his lips.

For a moment Jenny stared at him. She had accused him of things he didn't deny, and yet he kissed her hand. He was so confident. And why not? The court had accused her. She would die for the crime. She had hoped that somehow she might be wrong, that Tilden would say she was mistaken about his trying to murder her. But he made no denial.

Perhaps he knew she loved him enough to want him to live and be happy with her mother, rather than see him swing from the gallows.

"I will not say these things in a courtroom," she said, and with that, looked beyond Tilden to Bingham.

Tilden's fingers touched her face. "Oh, my dearest Jenny. What you must be going through."

She could bear his touch no longer, lest she beg him to hold her, to kiss her again, to lie and say he loved her. "How demented I must be," she cried aloud. "Oh, please, I must go."

Tilden rose and stepped aside. Standing before him, she could see the longing in his eyes. Perhaps his actions that night had been rash and he regretted it. But it was too late, all too late. With a cry, she turned and ran from the room.

Staring at the still-open door, Tilden contemplated Jenny's accusations. He thought of all the remarks he had made about Diane. He had said he would do anything for her. He had explained that his search for Jenny had been for Diane's sake. He had often spoken of Diane's beauty and of his admiration for her. He could readily see why Jenny concluded he was in love with her mother.

"She does not seem to realize, Tilden," Bingham said after a moment of quiet, "that you could have simply forgotten about her. No one else would have searched for her, and my firm would have done nothing without your prompting."

"So there goes my motive for attempting to murder Jenny?" Tilden asked, a wry grin playing about the corners of his mouth.

"Oh, we could press the point," Bingham replied. "A jury might even believe her to be right."

"As you have often said," Tilden commented, "the simplest, obvious things are usually the most generally overlooked."

Bingham nodded. "We're ready to go to trial," he announced.

"You are ready?" Only that morning Bingham had told him that he had not discovered the information he needed to properly defend Jenny.

"Yes," Bingham replied. "Tonight's conversation brought out things I should have anticipated."

"You do not mean, Bingham," Tilden asked, "that you believe I tried to murder Jenny?"

"You know that if I did, I would certainly present such evidence."

"That I know," Tilden remarked. "You can't actually believe. . .?"

A slow smile graced Bingham's lips, and a wizened look came into his eyes. "The evidence weighs heavily against you, Tilden. I think if these things came to light in a courtroom, as they did tonight, you most assuredly would be convicted."

Tilden stared. Finally a full smile spread across Bingham's face. "However, the important thing, Tilden, is what we have discovered tonight. The missing link. The key. The detail I've been looking for. That one piece of evidence."

"What is that?" Tilden asked, feeling strangely implicated.

"The poison was not intended for Lord Bodley. That is the only thing that can clear Jenny. We do not have to prove her innocence. We simply have to prove that the poison was not intended for Bodley."

"Even if the evidence is against me?"

"You hired me to clear her name, to prove her innocence, and that I shall do," Bingham said with a confidence Tilden had not detected before in this case. "Don't look so glum, old chap. If you didn't put the poison in the goblet, you have nothing to fear."

Astonished, Tilden inquired, "You think I did?"

"We must think as we would in a court of law, Tilden. As we did here tonight. You're a rising young attorney. Now, how does it look to you?"

Tilden snorted. "It looks as if I enticed Lady Jenny, kissed her to divert her attention, and gave her a poisoned drink so I could inherit all the duke's fortune and marry her mother." He half laughed with incredulity. "That is what the prosecuting attorney would point out, isn't it?"

"Exactly."

"And how do we answer?" Tilden asked.

"Simple," Bingham replied. "If you didn't do it, we quit trying to defend Jenny and begin to incriminate the real culprit."

"But as she said," Tilden pointed out, "no one else had a motive for wanting Jenny dead." He sat down and slumped in the chair, his forearms on his thighs, then straightened. "Bingham," he said slowly. "If Jenny really believes I tried to kill her, then why did she not mention it to you?"

Bingham smiled wryly. "To her, Tilden, you represent two

persons. Her first encounter with you was when you were simply a stranger, a knight in shining armor who offered her a means of escape from the intolerable present and hope for something other than an unbearable future. Then, when the stranger did not appear after she had been accused of murder, she believed the stranger had killed Bodley."

"But I did come to her, Bingham," Tilden replied. "Through you."

"She has not thought of it in that way, Tilden. She expected you personally. She never told me that you were the stranger."

"I am rather surprised at that," Tilden said.

Bingham shook his head. "No, Tilden. The stranger gave her a moment in her life that she had longed for and never had before. A moment to remember. I'm sure it has taken her a long time to face the facts that the stranger had not, shall we say, cared for her but was furthering his own selfish motives."

"I can see how it would look that way," Tilden said, beginning to understand. "Did she tell you those things about. . .a special moment in her life?" he asked, attempting to make his voice indifferent.

"No," Bingham said kindly. "It is something I have surmised by what she didn't say. Instinct, you might say."

"Instinct?"

"Yes, the same way I knew Jenny has been holding back something. As if protecting someone."

"Me," Tilden replied. "But why would she protect a murderer she felt was putting the blame on her or may even have tried to kill her?"

"As I stated, Tilden, you represent two people to her. You have been responsible for giving her the only sense of freedom she has ever had. She was hidden by her father and relatives. Here, she rides the grounds, sleeps when she wants, skips meals if she wishes, eats in her room, reads books without being ridiculed. She has servants rather than being one. Most important, you have reunited her with her mother. She cannot hate you. And she cannot publicly accuse you. I do think she would rather have her own life taken. I think if you tried to strangle her, she would not utter a single protest."

Surely Bingham exaggerated, and yet something about his words touched Tilden in a way nothing ever had. But he did not want some kind of unfounded gratitude from Jenny. He wanted much more. "I should go and talk to her," Tilden said, starting toward the doorway.

"Duke Tilden Withington!" Bingham's voice resonated in his most stern manner, and Tilden stopped short of the doorway. "Where were you the night Ignatius, Lord Bodley was murdered?"

Tilden stiffened and his gaze rested upon the door without seeing it. Instead, he saw possibilities that staggered his imagination with both horror and exhilaration.

"You know, Bingham," he replied levelly, neither his gaze nor his voice faltering, his back turned to Bingham.

"I've known all along," Bingham replied. "But why did you not tell me? Why did you allow so many weeks to pass without any word of your being in the glade with Jenny that night?"

Tilden had had many things on his mind the day after the murder. His first thoughts had been to prevent Jenny from being detained in a prison. Then he had been consumed with the idea of bringing Diane to her daughter. He had expected that Jenny herself would inform Bingham of all the events of that evening, including his having been there. He hadn't realized that he'd not told his name to Jenny. However, Bingham would have known who the stranger in the glade had to be. And regardless of what Jenny had said, there was no way of knowing if the arsenic had been in his glass or in Bodley's.

Bingham had asked his question the way it would be offered in the courtroom. He expected Tilden to give an accounting now, as he would later be forced to do in court.

"Why didn't I tell you, Bingham?" Tilden repeated after a long silence, feeling the attorney's eyes boring into his back. "Surely you cannot suspect that I would attempt to harm sweet Jenny."

Tilden turned, and his level gaze met the eyes of Silas Bingham. "There's only one reason, of course, that I followed Jenny into the glade that night," he confessed. "I'd searched for Lady Jenny for many years. Then when I found her, the most beautiful woman in the world, and discovered her engaged to that wretch, Bodley, I had no alternative. It was I who murdered Ignatius, Lord Bodley."

"That's ridiculous," Bingham said. "All you would have to do was whisk Jenny away from that party. She would have gone willingly. You had much more to offer than Bodley. You have no believable motive for murdering Bodley."

"Ah," Tilden said with a wry grin, "but you know the legends and myths surrounding the blood-thirsty Withingtons."

eleven

Jenny heard the news from Lady Diane. She had just finished breakfast in her dining area when Diane knocked, then burst in without waiting for an answer.

"Jenny," she said, rushing over to her. "Silas just told me. Tilden has confessed."

"Confessed?" Jenny rose to her feet, almost knocking over the small table. He admitted he tried to kill her? "You mean—?"

"Yes, yes, Darling. He says he murdered Bodley."

Jenny's thoughts were in turmoil. She had decided the poison had been intended for her and that Tilden had done it for the inheritance. Putting her hand to her head, she sank back into the chair.

"Oh, Mama, do you believe it?"

"Of course not, Jenny. Not any more than I believe you did it. I have come to the conclusion that you were framed. And Tilden?" She scoffed. "Why, he had no motive. He could buy and sell Bodley ten times over."

"Then why did he confess?" Jenny cried in desperation.

"For you, Jenny," she whispered in a shaking voice. "For you and for me."

"But you said nobody will believe him."

"Of course not! Not any more than I believe you murdered Bodley."

Jenny stared out the window. *Someone murdered him, though. The magistrate had me arrested for the murder. The court charged me with murder.*

"I must admit," her mother added, "this is a noble attempt on Tilden's part."

Jenny shook her head. Not noble, but clever. To divert attention from her accusation that she had been the intended victim, Tilden had confessed to a crime for which he knew he couldn't be convicted. And even if someone were to believe her claim—that he wanted her dead—he still wouldn't be convicted of murder because she hadn't died. His confession appeared so preposterous, she felt it made her look even guiltier.

Jenny put a shaking hand to her head. How unbearable to see her mother in such distress. Jenny realized that she alone stood in the way of her mother's happiness with Tilden. She would allow it no longer.

"I won't let him take the blame, Mama. I won't." She leaped from the chair and rushed out into the hallway, oblivious to her mother's pleas to let Bingham handle the situation.

Jenny ran to the study. Bingham wasn't there.

"Where is he?" she asked the butler.

"Who, My Lady?"

"Silas Bingham!"

"In his room, perhaps," the butler replied.

Jenny didn't know which room Bingham occupied during his stay at the castle. "Please direct me to his room," she ordered the butler, who registered surprise.

From years of training, he said nothing and bowed, then led the way to the west wing of the second floor. Jenny pounded on the door the butler pointed out. Almost immediately Bingham stood facing her.

"Protocol be hanged," he said, standing aside. "Come in."

Jenny stepped inside to find a valise on the bed.

"You're leaving?" she asked, her voice holding a note of terror.

"There's nothing more I can do here," he said resignedly, and she felt he looked a little older. But of course he would be distressed about Tilden's confession.

"You feel defeated, don't you?" she asked.

Bingham's eyes didn't meet hers, and she felt he deliberately turned away so she could not read his expression. When he turned back he had taken a shirt from the drawer and laid it in the valise.

"Because Til. . .Duke Withington. . .has confessed," she added.

"You could hardly expect me to be exuberant over such a matter," he replied curtly.

"No, of course not," she agreed and went over to sit on the edge of the bed so she could watch his face. "But he didn't do it. I did."

He stared at her, his face inscrutable. Then his face flushed with anger. "So! Both of you want to go to the gallows!" he stormed.

She had not seen him look like that before. He seemed hard and even cruel. She felt herself shrink away as he took a step closer, bending over her. "You two are bent upon destroying each other."

"No, no. He didn't have anything to do with it," she pleaded. "He must not be accused. I did it. Only I. You don't believe we did it together, do you?"

"Neither I, nor any court of law, believe you two were in cahoots. The kind of careful watch your relatives kept over you would prevent the opportunity for such plans to be put in effect."

"But it will only make me look more guilty if he confesses to the court. It will look like he believes I did it but is willing to take the blame. You will not allow Duke Withington to go through with this, wil! you?"

"Can I prevent him?"

"I am the one who is charged with the murder," she said, her voice rising. "I did it alone. No one helped me and no one else must be accused or allowed to confess. I will say it was my glass on that table beside Bodley's. I am guilty. I confess. I confess." With that, she buried her face in her hands.

A knock sounded on the door. "Pardon me," Tilden said, looking toward Jenny in surprise. He turned to Bingham. "I came to tell you the coach is ready whenever you are. Do you want to take me into town with you?"

"I take you in?" Bingham asked sullenly.

"Yes. I have confessed to murder. We need to do whatever is necessary to clear Jenny and take me into custody."

"But he can't take you in," Jenny interjected. "I have confessed to Mr. Bingham that I am guilty. We do not need to go to trial. I can be sentenced right away."

Silas Bingham shook his head. "If you two will excuse me, I will leave. There is important work to be done. But I will say, only one person is guilty of committing the crime and I intend to reveal that person's identity in trial. Neither of you is going to deny me that opportunity."

"Then you are certain who committed the crime?" Tilden asked.

"I haven't been sitting idly by, Tilden, waiting for confessions to come my way. That is not my method of operation."

"But I thought you were completely baffled," the duke replied, "until my confession."

"It might surprise you to learn I haven't disclosed all my findings to you, Tilden. It isn't a good practice since you are emotionally involved with some of the parties in question. Also, I've been aware that you concealed some vital facts from me."

"Then you intend to expose the villain during the trial?"

"That is what I just said, Tilden, and it is my usual practice. Sometimes I feel I missed my calling. Perhaps I should have gone on the stage. I do enjoy a good drama. Especially when I have the leading role." He closed the valise with a snap. "Please! Don't try and deprive me of earning the enormous fee this is costing you." His voice held a bit of humor and a smile hovered about his lips.

"Then you believe you know who the murderer is without a doubt?" Tilden asked.

"I know who and why," Bingham replied confidently. "Now I must discover how."

"Shall I tell you?" Tilden asked.

Bingham laughed softly and lifted a hand. "Please," he said, shaking his head. He then picked up the valise and headed for the door. "Leave a little work for me to do, Your Grace," he said mockingly. "How could I ever respect myself if my murderers tell me everything?"

He then grew serious as he studied both members of his bewildered audience. "There is something you two can do," he said. "I assure you the murderer will get his just dues, with or without confessions or protestations. So why don't you two stop trying to save each other and concentrate on telling the truth?"

Jenny didn't know the truth about anything anymore. Why did Bingham not take Tilden seriously? Were they all plotting against her—even Bingham? Or was Bingham planning a courtroom accusation of Tilden in court?

Bingham set the valise on the floor, then placed his hands on Tilden's and Jenny's shoulders. "Why don't you two concentrate on enjoying this short period of time before the trial? It begins in two weeks."

He then lifted the valise. A footman stood in the hall, ready to take it from him. As soon as Bingham was out of sight, Jenny said in a small voice, "Excuse me," and started to walk past Tilden.

His words stopped her progress. "Do you have a Bible in your room, Jenny?"

She felt her throat constricting. The question startled her as much as when the minister had asked if she wanted to repent.

Unable to speak, she took a few steps, saw Tilden's hand

move in her direction, then broke into a run down the long corridor.

≫

No one had mentioned the minister since that day when Jenny had run into the courtyard to rid herself of his words and had become drenched with the cold rain. Now she felt drenched with the tears that had fallen down her face throughout the day. She had refused to speak to anyone, except to insist that she would eat nothing.

As the day wore on, she began to see the futility of her inaction and remembered Bingham's words, "two weeks," and Tilden's question, "Do you have a Bible?" Those words implied impending doom.

If such were her future, should she not prepare herself? Or would she remain a whimpering wench with no backbone whatsoever? No one had been able to help her overcome this charge of murder. Bingham had tried, yet he refused to consider another person's confession. Her mother's belief in her innocence was based on hope, rather than hard evidence. After a sixteen-year absence, how could her mother possibly know her true character?

No one could help her. No one—in this world.

But could God? Would God? She did not know enough about Him. She thought Him fearful. And yet her mother had spoken of Jesus as someone wonderful that had come into her life.

Jenny arose from her bed of tears, bathed her face with cold water, and summoned Nellie. A short while later in her private dining room, while forcing herself to eat some of the sumptuous meal that had been brought up, she talked with her mother.

"I would like to apologize to the minister," she said, adding, "it was not he who made me run, but the fears within myself."

"We shall have him come again if you like," her mother

replied, hope shining in her eyes. "I shall instruct him to deliver his sermon on 'Love.' "

❧

To Jenny's surprise, the minister arrived before sunset. Although the small stone chapel felt cool, evening rays of the setting sun touched the stained glass windows and lent an ethereal glow to the small room. To her delight, the minister did not appear so ominous this time.

Sitting a few rows from the front, she did not know if anyone sat farther back, nor did it matter. She was not concerned about whether her innocence was believed; she wanted to know if she was prepared to face whatever fate awaited her.

The minister said that God loved the world so much He sent His Son, Jesus, to shed His blood and die for the sins of the world. All who believed in Him, repented of their sins, and accepted Jesus in their hearts, minds, and lives would be forgiven, would receive the Holy Spirit into their lives, and would live forever.

Jenny liked this sermon so much better than the few sermons she had heard in the past. They had made God seem so forbidding. But the minister made God seem approachable.

"We're all guilty of sin," the minister said. "Our thoughts condemn us. But there is hope. There is forgiveness. There is a new life possible for us—if we come to Jesus."

That's what her mother had said she and Tilden had done, Jenny realized. Obviously the experience had changed her mother's life. Although Jenny didn't like to think her mother had abandoned her to run away with Duke Stanford, she could understand how such a thing had happened when her mother was young, distressed, and so in love. But then she had begun a new life in Christ. And her mother had shown nothing but sorrow and repentance for the hurts Jenny had experienced during their long years of separation.

Then, a great shudder traveled through Jenny as a horrible

thought occurred to her. She too had been ready to do something reckless and sinful. During those terrible days when she was engaged to Bodley, she had been desperate enough that she herself might have been capable of murdering the man if the opportunity had arisen.

Even our thoughts condemn us, the minister said. At this moment, Jenny felt condemned not by a court, but by her own conscience and by the Word of God. She wanted to run as she had before. Something was telling her to flee. The glow had faded from the windows. Shadows crept. Darkness was falling. Words seemed to echo around the stone walls. "All have sinned. All have come short of the glory of God."

This feeling of guilt had nothing to do with the accusation of murder. It had nothing to do with whether anyone believed in her innocence. It had to do with her soul. Eternity loomed large before her. A higher court than man's had condemned her, and although she closed her eyes against the scene, she could not close her heart to the minister's words.

"The LORD is my shepherd; I shall not want."

I am to follow Him? Not want for anything? In this life. . .or in the next?

"He maketh me to lie down in green pastures: he leadeth me beside the still waters."

Oh, I want the green pastures, the still waters—not this impenetrable darkness.

"He restoreth my soul: he leadeth me in the paths of righteousness for his name's sake."

I want to run and hide, but at the same time I want to be restored. I want to be led along the right path.

"Yea, though I walk through the valley of the shadow of death, I will fear no evil: for thou art with me; thy rod and thy staff they comfort me."

I'm walking there, in the shadow of death. Not fear? Oh, I want that. I want a shepherd who will comfort me.

"Thou preparest a table before me in the presence of mine enemies: thou anointest my head with oil; my cup runneth over."

I have enemies who want to destroy me. But it is not the court of law that is my enemy. The real enemy is evil itself, is the sin that God says is in each person. This is an entirely different matter.

Jenny slipped from the bench, fell to her knees, and laid her head on the seat while rivers of troubled waters flowed from her eyes, like a fast-rushing stream cleansing the debris from its banks.

The minister's voice came nearer, but she did not mind. She was hearing God speak through his servant. "Surely goodness and mercy shall follow me all the days of my life: and I will dwell in the house of the LORD for ever."

The minister then added, "Jesus said, 'I am the good shepherd.' And also, 'him that cometh to me I will in no wise cast out.' Jenny, do you want this Good Shepherd to be your Lord and Savior?"

Do I want?

Slowly, Jenny raised her head and her tear-drenched face. Through eyes, blurred by tears, she saw the light. Had someone lit the candles in the wall niches? Or was it that her blinded eyes could now see?

With each flicker of the candle, alternating between shadow and light, her fear and doubt threatened, but she kept her eyes on the fuzzy glow and felt the words like a healing stream. "The Lord is my shepherd; I shall not want."

Do I want? Oh, I want for so much. I want the green pastures; I want the still waters; I want the restoring of my soul; I want the comfort; I want to dwell in the house of the Lord forever.

"Oh, yes," she whispered. Then the flood started again, and this time it flowed until she felt free and forgiven and clean and new, and she felt as if it were Jesus who lifted her to her feet.

"Then He is yours," the minister said. "He is with you in spirit and shall always be. You don't have to want for what He offers. It is now yours, for the taking."

"Now?" she asked. "Not just. . .in eternity?"

The minister smiled. "There is more in eternity. What you have now is His presence, His guiding, His comfort."

Even though I walk through the valley of the shadow of death, He is with me.

The minister prayed, and Jenny repented of the sin in her life, of all her mean, vindictive thoughts, even those she'd had against Bodley. She confessed those times when she'd had hard thoughts against her relatives, including her mother for abandoning her and her father for deceiving her, and against some of her governesses and tutors and even life itself.

Jenny felt as if the weight of her burden no longer weighed upon her. Oh, what would it be like—this new life?

Her mother was waiting outside the chapel door. "Oh, Mama, I too have Jesus in my heart," Jenny cried. But she didn't want to talk about it just then. She wanted to think about it, absorb it, and tell this Jesus all her troubles. The minister had said Jesus would be her Friend. She'd never really had a friend before. Now she wanted to get to know Him.

❧

Jenny had fallen asleep talking to her new Friend, after having read the first four books of the New Testament from Tilden's Bible. Her first words to her mother the following morning were, "I would like to be baptized."

"Oh, Jenny," her mother said, her eyes misty. "Nothing could be so satisfying to a mother than knowing her child has come into the kingdom of God." Jenny's mother had the minister summoned immediately.

Soon the minister, Jenny's mother, Tilden, Mrs. Millet,

Nellie, Nellie's mother, and as many of the household servants as could be spared, gathered in the small chapel on the castle grounds.

The morning sun shone softly on the stained glass windows, shedding prisms of jewel tones across the stone floor. The candles burning in their niches cast a golden glow over the stone walls and the faces of those who had gathered for this important event.

Jenny and the minister, he in a black robe and she in a white dress, faced the group who had gathered near the front of the chapel. Some brushed away tears, others let their tears roll freely. Some simply looked on with curiosity. Jenny's mother and Tilden stood near each other, and when a sob escaped the widow's throat, Tilden put his arm around her shoulders and drew her near.

Jenny noticed the action, and while it brought a sudden tug at her heart, she also experienced joy that they had each other. She could live without Tilden. But she could not live without Jesus. She now knew that there was no life without Him, only survival. With a radiant face, she looked over at the minister.

He spoke briefly about what had happened to Jenny the night before and informed the audience that salvation was available to each of them. Then lifting his hand, he said, "In obedience to our Lord's command, I baptize you, my sister, Jennifer Greenough, in the name of the Father, and of the Son, and of the Holy Ghost."

Jenny felt the cleansing waters of baptism, and when the ceremony was complete, she felt clean, inside and out. Her baptism symbolized a life dead to sin and guilt and risen again to a new life.

After the service, some of the onlookers sobbed openly as Jenny and the minister rejoined them. Jenny's mother had the group join hands and stand in a circle, and she drew Jenny in between herself and Tilden. Jenny had no choice but to take Tilden's outstretched hand. How warm and strong it felt, enclosing her smaller, colder one.

I shall not want, Jenny remembered. And accompanying her longing for Tilden was a willingness to let him go. Jesus would decide her future. She belonged to Him. She smiled as her mother led them in singing, "Oh God, Our Help in Ages Past," a song Jenny had heard the few times she had attended church.

Yes, she thought in wonder, *I love Him more—enough to want Tilden's happiness above my own.*

twelve

Jenny left the castle in the midafternoon. She walked outside in the bright sunlight that lent a golden glow to the trees and fields. Without bothering to see if attendants followed, she walked into the woods and sat on a bench where the sun filtered down upon her through branches almost devoid of leaves. Lost in reverie, she was oblivious to the falling of an occasional leaf around her and the breeze that stirred her dark hair, haloed by the sunlight.

Sensing the presence of someone, she gave a startled glance and then quickly lowered her gaze to her hands. A whisper of wind gently caressed the leaves.

When he spoke, Tilden's voice sounded deeper and lower than she had ever heard it. A most gentle sound. "I could not be more pleased by anything, Jenny," he said, "than what has taken place in your life."

She did not protest his presence when he sat beside her. Did he mean her having been accused of the murder, or did he mean her having given her life to the Lord? She drew her shawl closer and clutched it to her chest, suddenly made aware of her secluded surroundings.

She was afraid of him, but not because she thought he was a murderer. Something else disturbed her. Her foolish heart had learned no lesson from all the instruction her mind had given. Were he to touch her now, or kiss her, she would be unable to resist responding. Two weeks, she thought, might be all the freedom she had left. Inhaling deeply, she gazed ahead of her at a falling leaf.

"No one believes you killed Bodley," she said quietly. "Mama does not. Bingham does not."

"They will," he stated firmly. "Should I make such a confession in court, it cannot be ignored. When I make it known that I attended the party, there will be those who will remember seeing me and realize my absence later in the evening. That will condemn me, Jenny."

"And what is your motive now?"

"You," he replied. "It will not be difficult at all for anyone to believe I could not bear for Bodley to have you. I could tell such a thing quite convincingly."

Jenny felt ill at ease, not wishing for anyone to commit a terrible crime, but wishing it were true that he could love her so much he couldn't bear for Bodley or anyone else to have her. But she must stop her fantasizing and focus on reality. "Why would you do such a thing?"

He remained silent.

"How do you know I didn't kill him?" she asked finally.

"If you did," he replied, "you would not believe that I killed Bodley, nor would you have feared that I had made an attempt on your life."

"I'm. . .not sure you did it," she murmured. She heard his intake of breath, but would not look at him. Her voice softened. "If you didn't, then you must despise me."

"I could never despise you, Jenny," he replied quickly, and she felt his warm breath against her cool cheek. "But I want to ask something of you."

Jenny turned her head to look at him and feared she would never look away. She became lost in his gaze, a look that she felt should be reserved for someone special. She could not even find the words to ask him what he wanted of her. Then he took her hands in his.

"I want you to grant me the privilege of your company for the next two weeks, Jenny. Surely you can find it in your heart to grant this to a man who may have only two weeks of freedom left."

How could she say that would be no sacrifice, but a wonderful blessing? How could she say that she understood Bathsheba better than any other woman in the world? She could not, even when she watched Tilden's expression turn to pain. He let go of her hands, stood dejectedly, and turned away. She watched him walk several paces into the woods, with his back to her.

Wondering if she were the world's most foolish woman, Jenny stopped asking herself whether or not Tilden had a murderous heart, whether or not he had fallen in love with her mother. Whatever he had done, she forgave him, just as Bathsheba must surely have forgiven King David.

She lifted her skirt, stepped gingerly over the fallen leaves and twigs, and approached Tilden's back. If he had committed the murder, he did not do it as a cold-blooded killer but to save her from Bodley and reunite her with her mother. In the two weeks remaining of her personal freedom, she would spend time with the man she loved. God had allowed her to fall in love with him in that glade. Surely a reason existed for this, even if it were only that she know love, its joy and pain, for this short period of time. She had been at the residence of the man she loved for many weeks now. He had made them the happiest of her life. She would live in fear and sorrow no longer.

As he heard the sound of Jenny's footsteps on the leaves, Tilden held his breath. He became aware of the scent she wore, the fragrance that haunted his dreams. His muscles stiffened when she touched his arm. Afraid to look upon her, he placed his hand over hers and turned. The realization of his emotional turmoil struck him with full force.

He recalled the Scripture, *For as he thinketh in his heart, so is he*, and called upon the Lord's strength to keep him from yielding to this moment of dire temptation.

"Jenny, Jenny," he moaned and drew her to his chest in an embrace that he could remember when he was alone. But for now, as one who had committed his life to the Lord, he must resist. One arm encircled her waist and the other hand spread its fingers to reach into her hair and feel the nape of her neck. Her soft skin felt warm beneath his touch.

"I do not trust myself where you are concerned," he admitted. "Despite what I might say, please have the attendants accompany us from now on. Otherwise I fear my actions shall be most unbecoming a gentleman. Promise me that."

Jenny looked up to find his chin directly above the top of her head. His wide, full lips were tightly closed, his facial muscles taut, his eyes closed against some unwanted intrusion. His fingers moved against her neck.

She could not know if he feared he might strangle her, or if he might kiss her. She was tempted to tell him that if he must strangle her, please kiss her first. But of course, she could not say such a thing. So, because he asked, and afraid of the fierce beating of her heart, she replied helplessly, "I promise."

He seemed so distressed. Jenny moved away from him, and his arms fell to his side. In silence the couple walked through the rustling leaves, amid the gentle whisper of the wind, toward the castle.

❧

Jenny and Tilden rode together each morning, across the fields and through the meadows, pausing by the lake to regard its beauty and the stillness of the world. Time flew. Jenny enjoyed every moment. She detected not a trace of jealousy from her mother, who seemed to encourage Jenny's activities with Tilden.

The evenings were the best. Sometimes Jenny's mother joined them in the library for discussions of whatever novel Jenny was reading, but usually she did not. She always gave excuses of having other household duties to attend to.

Many times after a fire had been lit to dispel the chill of an autumn evening, Jenny and Tilden settled by the cozy hearth and discussed books and ideas, life and death. Jenny was fascinated by the eloquent and convincing way in which Tilden stated his belief in Christianity.

"In this belief, this acceptance," Tilden said emphatically, "you have found the answer to life, Jenny. No amount of money or knowledge can buy it, nothing can compare with it, and nothing can take it away."

"Oh, thank you, Tilden," she breathed happily. "Thank you so much for having the minister come and for lending me your Bible. I shall be eternally grateful."

"Yes," he said. "You and I shall spend eternity together."

She felt eternity had arrived as they gazed at each other while the orange light of the fire leaped to dispel the shadows. Jenny realized something new had been added to her love for Tilden. She felt more depth to it—a greater love. Perhaps an unselfish love that wanted his happiness, even if it could not be found with her.

❧

Jenny wondered what the last night before the trial would be like. Would Tilden kiss her, even in a brotherly way? Should she reveal her love for him?

A lifetime of living had been done over the past few months. She had come to accept the living Jesus in her heart. She had been reunited with her mother. She had loved a man with all the love she was capable of. She began to feel that if God wanted her to be free, she would. If not, she would try to be brave and accept the verdict. But she would not have to go to trial alone. Jesus promised His presence would always be with her. God had not spared His own Son suffering and death. He might not spare her either. But in the midst of her fear, she felt a supernatural peace.

After dinner the night before the trial, Jenny, Tilden, and her mother had tea in the library. No words were forthcoming, until Jenny's mother said she felt tired, begged to be excused, and retired to her rooms. The tension lay heavily upon Jenny's heart.

Tilden stood and walked over to the fireplace and faced Jenny. "There is so much in my heart I would like to say to you, Jenny," he began. "But it must wait. Perhaps it can never be said. Tomorrow is a day of truth. I find that most exhilarating and at the same time dreadful."

She lifted her eyes to his, and they told him she felt similar emotions about the inevitable day of truth.

"Jenny, I have become so much involved in your life, that mine seems meaningless in comparison. You have always been my project. Most of my life has been taken with longing for you to be with your mother, wishing you well, searching for you, and now. . ." He paused, closed his eyes for a moment, then continued. "I struggled for a long time before I concluded that without you, my life is half a life."

"You are so noble," she whispered.

He shook his head. "No, I am a coward," he contradicted. "There is so much I wish to say to you. But I must say no more. I mustn't. Your heart is burdened with more than any young woman should have to bear. There are more pressing matters at the moment than my personal feelings. I will only say that I shall be beside you in this. I shall always be with you, even when I am not present. But I must stop. I do not trust myself to spend this evening with you. I must go."

Jenny didn't move. Tilden did not go. The moisture in his eyes matched that which raced down her cheeks.

"Please go, for I cannot," he said in a raspy voice. He was afraid to look upon her lovely countenance aglow in the fire-light, yet he could not take his gaze away from her.

"Tilden," she breathed, standing, then took a step toward him.

"Please," he implored.

With a sob in her throat, Jenny turned and ran from the room. Reaching her mother's door, she knocked, and as soon as it opened she fell into her mother's arms. Her mother led her to a couch, held her head against her heart, and stroked her hair for a very long time, just as she had done when Jenny had been a very little girl.

thirteen

They left the castle at dawn. Jenny, her mother, and Tilden rode in the white carriage with the golden trim, drawn by the magnificent horses. The carriage that followed them down the winding paths and through the sleepy little village held Tilden's secretary, Diane's maid, Nellie, and Mrs. Millett.

Jenny could not resist asking Tilden to have the coachman stop the carriage outside the village so she could look back at the castle. She stood for a long moment outside the carriage, Tilden beside her, and stared at the pink sky being turned to gold by the sun. There, upon the cliffs, high above the sea, she had spent the happiest moments of her life. She had gained more in the past two weeks than she could ever have imagined. Memories were something no one could take from her. Already, she had eternal life and would be with her Savior forever. And as long as she lived on earth, she would have the memories of spending time with the man, the only man, that she could ever love.

Feeling the pressure of Tilden's hand as he grasped hers, Jenny knew the time had come to go. They mustn't dally. This was the day of truth, Bingham had said.

The carriages rolled over the open countryside, and the passengers commented upon the views, enjoying the ride as if it were a wonderful outing. Jenny marveled at the courage of the human spirit, for she knew how emotionally unpredictable she had proved to be during the past months. God's Spirit within had enabled her to bear such uncertainty.

Despite their heavy burdens, the threesome spoke lightly of the beauty of London as they neared its famous bridge in the early morning light. Jenny barely glanced at the court-house when she alighted from the carriage, concentrating instead on Bingham, who was waiting for them. He wore the traditional white powdered wig and dark robes of a barrister. She expected him to take her to a side room for instruction, but he appeared quite unconcerned, saying only, "Remember to answer truthfully, whatever questions are asked of you."

"I shall be praying for you every moment, my darling," Jenny's mother whispered as she gave her a last encouraging hug.

The courtroom began to fill. A matron escorted Jenny to the prisoner's dock, where she would stand throughout the trial. Looking straight ahead, she observed the juror's box, where the men who would decide her fate would be seated. The judge's high bench stood against the wall to her right, and the witness box was located beside it. Bingham and the prosecuting attorneys sat at long tables across from the jury.

Jenny looked around the courtroom and noticed that Tilden and her mother sat in the front row of the public seating. They smiled encouragingly. She watched as the Cottinghams arrived and walked down the aisle. Sir Thomas's face began to redden with apparent surprise at seeing Jenny's mother. Lady Christine's face paled, as if she were seeing someone long departed.

Jenny watched her mother look at them with an air of dignity, showing no sign of the shame that might be expected from a woman who had abandoned her daughter and now watched that daughter stand accused of murder. It was the Cottingham family who appeared embarrassed and hurried past to take their seats on the left side of the courtroom.

Soon, the somber jurors filed in. Everyone stood for the judge's entrance. The day of truth had arrived.

After several witnesses gave their account of the engagement party at Bodley's, Bingham called Emmaline to the stand. Twisting a lacy white handkerchief, her cheeks the color of her pink dress, she reiterated that she didn't believe Jenny would have done those terrible things she had threatened to do, although Jenny always read novels, had a wild imagination, opposed what she called the "marriage market," swore she hadn't meant to steal her cousin's intended, and really wouldn't hurt a flea.

Emmaline presented such an impression of a pure, innocent maiden who had expected Lord Bodley to ask for her hand in marriage, that Jenny felt she, herself, must truly look like a villain in comparison. Someone must have coached Emmie to pretend she loved Lord Bodley, so she wouldn't be suspected of taking the rash action of a woman scorned.

The real surprise, however, occurred when Tilden was called to the stand to testify about what he had seen at the party.

"You were a friend of Ignatius, Lord Bodley?" Bingham asked.

"An acquaintance," Tilden quickly amended. "We had mutual friends, and each time I visited London, we were inevitably present at various functions."

"I believe that your mutual friends were primarily in royal circles, is that correct?"

"It is," Tilden replied.

"Why, might I ask, did you follow Miss Jennifer Greenough into the glade?"

"I sought her out to inform her of the recent inheritance that my brother, the late Duke Stanford Withington, had left to her."

"Did you so inform her?"

"No," he replied. "I promised to see her the following day but left the glade hurriedly upon hearing Bodley approach, rather than risk an unpleasant confrontation with a man I knew was already under the influence of alcohol. After all, it was their engagement party. And if I were engaged to one such as Lady Jennifer Greenough, I would not take kindly to her presence with another man in a secluded glade."

Bingham waited until a trickle of understanding laughter and comments from the onlookers dissipated before he continued. "Were you in London the night that the father of the accused, William, Lord Greenough, died eight years ago?"

"Yes, I was in London during that time, and on that particular night," Tilden admitted.

Jenny didn't understand why Bingham was referring to the night her father died and what connection it had with this trial. But Bingham had said he suspected there was a connection between the two. Before she could make any sense out of the situation, Bingham excused Tilden. Then Jenny's aunt Christine sat in the witness box.

"Would you say, Lady Cottingham," Bingham asked, "that your brother drank himself to death?"

The woman seemed uncertain how to answer. She appeared surprised to be questioned about her brother.

"Lady Cottingham, please answer the question," Bingham insisted in a quiet voice.

"That was reported as the cause of death," she replied stiffly, not meeting the eyes of anyone in the courtroom. "Sir Thomas and I spoke with him many times concerning the welfare of little Jenny. And yes, I must admit, he was gambling, wasting his money, and did indeed imbibe the spirits almost continually."

"He drank from a glass, I assume?"

Jenny's aunt lifted her chin nobly, and her lower lip quivered magnificently. "I'm afraid my brother did not bother with glasses," she said quietly.

"That will be all," Bingham said so abruptly the entire courtroom was stunned into complete silence.

❧

Tilden felt the tension building. With Bingham playing the

leading role, this became not only a legal proceeding, but a performance. The spectators always expected something extraordinary from Bingham, but this case appeared impossible to figure. A total absence of anything spectacular being revealed gave the event a more ominous air. Even the prosecutor kept saying, "No questions," as if the comments of Bingham's defense witnesses were quite insignificant.

If Tilden hadn't known better, he would have suspected Bingham had lost his touch, for the famous attorney kept dwelling on an event that took place eight years ago rather than on the present tragedy. The duke knew that eventually Bingham would target the culprit, but when? And on whom?

Suddenly Bingham called Jenny to the stand.

⁂

Emmaline thought Jenny looked older than twenty-one. She supposed such experiences as her cousin had endured over the past few months matured a person, but Jenny should have remembered the oft-repeated instructions they'd received: Young ladies wear pink and white. Instead, Jenny had dressed in a bright green velvet dress with a tight-fitting jacket, giving her the look of a mature woman.

The sun suddenly burst forth outside the window, as if to drive away the chill of the autumn morning. Its rays touched Jenny's hair, turning the long raven tresses to a burnished sheen of reddish-gold. Jenny seemed to belong to the summer in that green dress, appearing alive and growing in the sun. Emmaline's mother had said young girls shouldn't allow the sun to touch their skin. Jenny looked as if she hadn't obeyed. Even her cheeks had the blush of the sun on them.

Emmaline shifted her gaze to Lady Diane. Right after they had taken their seats, Emmaline had asked her father, "Who is the woman who looks so much like Jenny?"

"Her mother," he replied.

Emmaline had been under the impression that Jenny's

mother was dead. Now as she studied Lady Diane, Emmaline noticed the woman had a sad, sweet smile on her lips. She wore the clothes of a true lady and gazed upon Jenny as if she approved of her wholeheartedly.

Emmaline lowered her head, examining her soft white fingers. Her mother had been right. Jenny was very much like her mother.

❧

Jenny sat in the witness box, distressed as Bingham began painting a vivid word picture of her—the poor motherless child who had been abandoned. She glanced at her mother helplessly, not wanting her to be embarrassed, but her mother's gaze showed only love, warmth, and encouragement.

At Bingham's bidding, Jenny related her loneliness and that her father had told her that her mother was dead. She told of her father's drinking and how she would hide when he drank, although she found him quite loving when he was sober.

"Do you recall the events that surrounded your going to live with Sir Thomas and Lady Cottingham?"

"Yes, sir," Jenny replied. "My father and I had recently moved to London. Uncle Thomas and Aunt Christine came to talk with my father. He had already agreed that I should go to live with my aunt and uncle. I thought he needed me, but he told me I must go and learn to be a proper lady. He cried, and I felt he really cared about me then."

Tears welled up in Jenny's eyes, but she blinked them away, sniffed, and looked at Silas Bingham.

"Continue," he demanded, and she did, although not understanding why he didn't get to the point of the trial.

"That night, Aunt Christine told me that I would be leaving to go and live with them. My father came up to my room with a bottle in his hand, drinking and mumbling something like, 'What else can I do?' He lifted his hands helplessly and then left."

Jenny swallowed hard and grew pale. "It was the next morning that I found my father in the kitchen, slumped over a table. I could not awaken him. That was not so unusual, but when Aunt Christine and Uncle Thomas came down, they summoned a doctor. Later, it was disclosed that my father had drunk himself to death."

"How old were you then, Jenny?" Bingham asked.

"Thirteen."

Bingham turned to his audience. "The records show that Lady Jennifer's father died of excessive drinking. Once they discovered that he had signed away his assets, including his daughter, to the Cottinghams in case of his demise, the authorities assumed the poor man had nothing to live for. After all, the world knew he had been deserted by one of the most beautiful women about. He had lost his seat in Parliament because of the scandal. Why shouldn't the poor man have drunk himself to death?"

Then Bingham gestured toward Jenny. "Take a look at this sweet young girl."

Jenny felt herself blush and looked down at her clasped hands resting on her green velvet dress. Bingham's words didn't sound complimentary. He had become like a total stranger, incapable of any softness. She grew quite afraid. All eyes were upon her.

"She doesn't look like a woman to be thrown into prison," Bingham continued. "She's much too lovely. A beautiful maiden. An abandoned child. One first hidden away, then thrust away by her father, who apparently preferred the bottle to his own daughter. Now, ladies and gentlemen," Bingham said in a tone of mockery, "I submit that this girl may not be all that she appears to be."

Jenny's eyes flew to Bingham in surprise. All other eyes left her and centered on Bingham. He became the sole actor on the stage. He was apparently accusing his own client of. . .what?

Bingham appeared to be enjoying himself. "The reports are that on the morning of the investigation of Lord Greenough's death, there was in front of him one bottle and one glass with a powdery ring around it. Dregs of a cheap beverage, perhaps?

"Yet two witnesses, one the accused, the other the sister of the deceased, have testified that Lord Greenough drank from bottles, not glasses. Would he, a defeated man on the night of having lost everything, suddenly have begun drinking from a glass? Why? To celebrate his failures? After so many years, did his adversities suddenly make a gentleman of him? Why would Lord Greenough take a glass on the night of his most dismal defeat? He drowned himself in liquor that night. Deliberately, knowing his system could take no more. Suicide, they said."

Some shook their heads, not knowing the answer but waiting for Bingham's explanation. Jenny was hearing the facts of her father's death for the first time. She too stared at the man before her, waiting for his answers.

"Could it be," Bingham asked in ominous tones, "that someone. . .someone. . .came down after everyone else fell asleep that night, found this man in his misery, and pretended to comfort him? Perhaps this *friend* even took a goblet and poured the poor defeated man a drink to show his sympathy. Perhaps the *friend* even slipped a little something into the goblet which left a powdery ring. Something such as. . ." Bingham paused and gazed around the assembly, making sure every eye was upon him. "Arsenic!" he finished.

No one seemed to breathe. Bingham looked at Jenny in his accusatory manner, and were she not so surprised by his behavior, she would have withered and completely disappeared.

"Could it be?" he questioned with authority, sweeping his gaze over every pair of eyes turned upon him. "Could it be that this sweet young girl, even at age thirteen, had murderous instincts? Could she, who had been abandoned by her mother, who had hidden from her father, who was now being given away like so much baggage, have put arsenic in that drink which left a powdery ring just like that on the glass in the glade where Ignatius, Lord Bodley met his untimely death?"

Immediately the silence in the courtroom was replaced by a roar. The judge banged his gavel, but neither that action nor his threats to clear the courtroom made any impact on the commotion for several minutes. Bingham appeared to be accusing his client, not of one murder, but of two. Jenny's sweet countenance had changed to a mask of incredulity. Stunned into compliance, she dutifully allowed Bingham to take her arm and lead her back to the dock.

fourteen

Later in the day, murmurs sounded throughout the crowded courtroom when the beautiful, elegant Lady Diane sat in the witness box. She wasn't the picture of a woman who had lived a life of shame. Rather she sat with dignity, as one who had endured many trials. From the moment she began to speak, she held her audience spellbound. Her words rang true.

Bingham went back further with his questioning than he had with any other witness. He asked about Lady Diane's first marriage and subsequent events. Her story flowed from her as if it had been waiting many years to be revealed.

She told about the forced marriage, the beautiful baby who gave her a reason to live, the jealous, angry husband, the love she had for Duke Stanford Withington. She told of her husband's mistreatment and ultimate abuse of Jenny. Finally, she revealed that she had signed over all her possessions to her husband in exchange for his promise of a divorce, only to discover he had no intentions of keeping his word.

She sought the duke's help, and he booked passage on a ship to America. They planned their departure during a week when Lady Cottingham, Sir Thomas, and little Emmaline were visiting the Greenoughs. Lady Diane and Jenny would sneak away in the middle of the night with the aid of a manservant.

Lady Diane recalled being surprised by how easily they had managed to get away. No one seemed suspicious of their actions that day. Lady Diane had given Jenny a small amount of sleeping draught to keep her from awakening and making noise. The manservant had taken the sleeping child, covered by a blanket, to an appointed spot in the woods where Stanford and Tilden were waiting.

Tilden had held the sleeping child in the back of a carriage while Stanford, with Diane beside him, drove the carriage to the docks where their freedom lay. Stanford, who had never before seen Jenny, tucked the child away in a reserved cabin. Then he, Diane, and Tilden kept to the adjoining cabin, alert to any disturbance that might indicate their plot had failed.

When the ship moved out onto the water, they breathed more easily. They were on their way to a new world, and a new life.

Early in the morning Diane went in to check on the sleeping child, who still had not stirred. She screamed in agony. The child sleeping peacefully beneath the blanket was not her darling Jenny, but rather Emmaline Cottingham.

Stanford rushed into the room and unfastened the envelope tied to the little girl's dress. He had read the letter to Diane.

At that point in the proceedings, Lady Diane looked at Bingham for confirmation and then unfolded a worn piece of paper. She read it aloud to the courtroom.

Authorities will be awaiting this child at the next port. She must leave the ship assisted only by ship personnel, without any trouble from you, or you will be arrested and prosecuted for kidnaping. Any attempts to do otherwise will result in an extended and losing battle on your part. I do not intend to relinquish Jenny to an adulterous and conniving woman (whose sins will be known throughout Europe) nor to the good-for-nothing duke who would take advantage of another man's wife.

I hope you understand. To disgrace you publicly as you have disgraced me would bring me great satisfaction. Any attempt to leave the ship at the next port will

*result in both you and the duke being prosecuted and
thrown into prison.*

> *Your choice, my dear,*
> *Your loving husband, Wm.*

Lady Diane folded up the paper and continued her story.
When she and the Withington brothers had come into port at
another point along the coast of England, authorities came
aboard ship, requesting that the little blond girl be released.
They had been alerted that a kidnaping had taken place. The
distraught parents had agreed that if the kidnapers would
release the child and continue on to America, no charges of
kidnaping would be lodged.

Diane and Stanford had no alternative but to return little
Emmaline Cottingham to her parents, who were watching the
ship, wringing their hands, and weeping.

Diane, Stanford, and Tilden had known it would be useless
to explain that they were the victims of a hoax created by
Diane's husband, using the Cottinghams as accomplices.
They were legally helpless to ever get Jenny. Their only hope
had been to somehow find her and take her away from her
father. All their efforts to that end had been futile.

Jenny looked over at the Cottinghams. Emmaline stared at
her mother, her mouth agape, but Lady Christine did not rep-
rimand her. She merely stared at the far wall. Sir Thomas
took his silver snuff box from his pocket, sniffed a pinch,
then replaced it.

Jenny then turned her gaze back to her mother, who had
held her audience's attention, even moving them to tears. It
was the first time Jenny had heard the reason she and her
mother had been separated for all those years. She had forgiven her mother for whatever the reason and loved her
dearly, but this turn of events made things all the more wonderful, for her mother had not willingly abandoned her.

"Mama," Jenny whispered as her mother passed by her. The woman smiled at Jenny through her tears. Looking back, Jenny saw that Tilden had time to give her mother a discreet hug around the shoulders before Bingham recalled him to the witness box.

"It would seem," Bingham began as soon as Tilden took his seat, "that the crimes and deception began long before Lord Bodley was murdered, and the evidence points to the fact that all the incidents are related to or revolve around Miss Jennifer Greenough. Could it be," Bingham asked mockingly, "that the five-year-old Jenny plotted this latest incident of which we have learned?"

A trickle of ironic laughter filled the courtroom. Bingham had asked the question in the same way he had asked if Jenny had murdered her father. He seemed to be showing the fallacy of anyone suspecting his client of murder, for she must be guilty of conspiracy in all the incidents—or in none.

"Or," he continued, as even the jurors sat on the edge of their seats, "was this young lady a victim at the age of five, when her aunt and uncle engaged in such deception, substituting their own child for Lady Jennifer Greenough?"

"Objection, your honor," the prosecuting attorney said, but was overruled when Bingham presented the note Diane had read. The handwriting had already been verified by an expert as the handwriting of Lord William Greenough.

"Now, I am not arguing that Lady Diane Greenough was right and Lord William Greenough was wrong," Bingham assured his audience. "The custody of the child should have been a matter for the courts. However, I think it perfectly fitting to present the case that the Cottinghams entered into a deceptive and illegal practice in substituting their child for Lady Greenough's and withholding Lady Greenough's own child from her, where the child had every right to be. It could well be the Cottinghams who might be accused of kidnaping.

And I submit further, that the deception embarked upon that night has continued throughout the years when the Cottinghams repeatedly told Lady Jennifer Greenough that her mother had died."

Bingham suddenly turned toward Tilden, in the witness box. "Duke Withington, who stood to profit by the death of Lord William Greenough, if anyone?"

"Lady Jennifer Greenough stood to profit financially," Tilden answered, "until shortly before Lord Greenough's death, when he signed over his assets to Sir Thomas and Lady Christine Cottingham. They had access to the holdings of Lord Greenough and the authority to distribute his wealth as they wished as long as Lady Jennifer remained their ward."

"And in what manner was the money to be spent? Were there stipulations?" Bingham asked pointedly.

"Lady Greenough's basic needs were to be met, including her education. Also, the death of Lord Greenough came at a most convenient time for them, because his money saved Sir Thomas Cottingham from bankruptcy. Lord Greenough's assets were considerable and included the funds Lady Diane had signed over to her husband in return for the divorce he wouldn't give. The Cottinghams have lived off Lady Jenny's money for the past eight years."

Jenny's surprised glance darted toward her aunt and uncle. She had wanted many things during that time. Simple things really. And she had longed for either a more competent tutor or the opportunity to be sent away to school.

Emmaline was biting on her nails and crying. Lady Christine's head was lowered, as if in defeat. She stared fixedly at her clasped hands. Sir Thomas appeared rather dazed, like a man humiliated, as he stared at Tilden.

"And who would gain if Ignatius, Lord Bodley were dead?" Bingham continued.

"No one, Sir," Tilden replied immediately.

"And who would gain if Lady Jennifer Greenough were dead? If the poison were intended for her?"

Jenny held her breath. Was Bingham now going to accuse Tilden of trying to murder her? She could hardly believe the words Tilden said when he answered.

"No one, Sir. We would all be the losers if Lady Jennifer Greenough should not grace this world with her beauty and charm."

Bingham cleared his throat as a few chuckles sounded through the courtroom. "I mean, Your Grace, who would benefit financially if Lady Jennifer were murdered?"

"I and her mother, Sir, for we would inherit all of Duke Stanford's estate, rather than share it with Lady Jennifer."

A murmur traveled through the courtroom, and the judge threatened to empty it if silence wasn't restored immediately.

"Tell us, Your Grace," Bingham entreated Tilden, "how you happened to be at the party, and in the glade, the night Lord Bodley drank his poisoned drink."

Jenny's thoughts were in turmoil. It seemed that everything was leading to Bingham accusing Tilden of trying to murder her so he could get the bulk of the inheritance.

"I had spoken with Sir Thomas Cottingham a week before," Tilden explained, and Jenny again looked at her relatives. Both Emmaline and Aunt Christine appeared surprised.

"All had been settled concerning my brother's estate. I felt it time I left Lady Diane in America and tried to see Lady Jennifer. We had known for several years the whereabouts of Lady Jenny but had received letters to the effect that she did not wish to see her mother or have any contact with her. We now know these letters were forgeries, in the handwriting of Lady Christine Cottingham."

Bingham presented the bundle of letters—those written to Jenny and returned, as well as those written by Lady Christine Cottingham.

"Then when Lady Jennifer inherited part of my brother's estate," Tilden continued, "I thought it time to confront her personally, for if she still rejected her mother, surely she would not reject the money and property."

"And did you see her?"

"No," Tilden replied. "Sir Thomas informed me that she was too busy preparing for her engagement party and that she soon would be married. He invited me to the engagement party."

Sir Thomas calmly pinched his snuff from the silver box, then replaced it in his pocket.

"Most sporting of him," Bingham remarked.

"Indeed," Tilden replied.

"And did you tell Lady Jennifer Greenough of her inheritance?"

"I followed her to the glade for that purpose," Tilden replied, looking at Jenny. "But we were interrupted."

"By Lord Bodley?" Bingham asked.

After a pause, Tilden answered, "Yes."

Suddenly Bingham wore the look that Tilden, the judge, and most of the occupants of the courtroom always waited for. It indicated that the moment for his startling revelation had arrived. Tilden stared at Bingham uncomfortably and felt himself growing quite warm. It was as if he were guilty and about to be accused and convicted.

Bingham did not, however, accuse Duke Tilden Withington of murder, or even attempted murder. Instead he simply asked the duke to step down. Then Bingham called Sir Thomas Cottingham to the stand.

Sir Thomas answered Bingham's questions in the same controlled modulated tone in which they were asked, even stopping on occasion to take a pinch of snuff. The questions were of a general nature, pertaining to his relationship with Jenny and the years of her upbringing. Sir Thomas, of course, had every legal right to her money, had provided for her basic needs, and therefore had nothing to fear from the law on that count. The fact that Jenny had been treated as a poor relation remained an ethical question, not a legal one, and was mentioned only in a passing remark by Bingham, as if it were inconsequential. The jury, however, seemed to take note of his words.

"It really isn't necessary to investigate your deceit, Sir Thomas, the night you substituted your young daughter for little Jenny. I don't believe anyone would care to press charges on that matter at this late date."

Sir Thomas had the presence of mind not to reply.

"But the matter of Lord Greenough's death is a different matter," Bingham said with concern. "There's this old doctor who said he got to thinking afterwards about that white powdery ring around that glass. He suspected it came from something other than an alcoholic beverage, but then he told himself the man no doubt committed suicide. Why, the doctor wondered, should he bring such scandal upon the poor child, on top of everything else she had to endure? But," Bingham drawled slowly, as if his words were of little importance, "it might be difficult to prove at this late date, would not you agree, Sir Thomas?"

Sir Thomas shrugged. "I certainly have no reason to believe my brother-in-law died of anything but his drinking," he replied. "However, I can see that the conditions of his life could cause him to sink to suicide."

Bingham shook his head, and Sir Thomas looked away from his eyes and fixed his stare on a distant wall. "I think murder is a more appropriate word," Bingham said simply. "More appropriate than suicide."

Suddenly he faced Sir Thomas, asking quickly, "Would you benefit by the death of Ignatius, Lord Bodley?"

"There is no reason whatsoever that I would want Bodley

dead," Sir Thomas answered confidently, sitting a little straighter in the chair and looking directly at Bingham. "I, personally, would have greatly benefitted by the marriage of Bodley and my ward."

"In what way?" Bingham asked quietly, turning his back on Sir Thomas and looking out at his audience with what might be mistaken for a smug look of satisfaction.

Sir Thomas told in detail of the deal between him and Bodley. His every word seemed to exonerate him of any suspicion of his motives, had any ever existed. Legal papers had been drawn up with his and Bodley's signatures. Sir Thomas presented the papers that proved he would have benefitted more by the marriage of Bodley and Jenny than by any transaction he had ever made.

"It would certainly appear that Sir Thomas Cottingham had no motive whatsoever to murder Lord Bodley," Bingham agreed. "There isn't a shred of evidence to point in that direction."

Just as Sir Thomas got a self-satisfied look on his face, Bingham turned toward him and continued. "I believe we have every reason to suspect Sir Cottingham in the murder of Lord Greenough, but of course that is not a question for this trial."

Sir Thomas closed his eyes. He made no sound, and his face was set as in stone, revealing nothing. Lady Christine, however, looked briefly concerned, sitting near the front and studying her husband. Then she took a deep breath, straightened her shoulders, and raised her chin imperiously.

The silence in the courtroom was broken by Bingham's quiet voice. "No," he said, "I don't for a moment think you would murder Bodley. Nor do I think the poison was intended for Lady Jenny."

Sir Thomas's eyes came up to meet Bingham's.

"No," Bingham repeated, shaking his head.

Sir Thomas tried to look away, but he didn't seem able to

move. "Could I have a glass of water?" he finally asked.

"That's the least we can do," Bingham replied, without taking his eyes from Sir Thomas. The witness had grown quite red and sweat covered his forehead.

"Bring a glass of water," Bingham ordered, without addressing anyone in particular.

Complete silence permeated the room during the eternity in which the glass of water was fetched. During the silence, Jenny stared at her uncle Thomas questioningly. She could not comprehend what she knew to be taking place. She was afraid to even speculate as she watched the clerk bring the water to Sir Thomas.

Bingham waited while Sir Thomas took a swallow of water and then set the glass on the wooden railing beside him. Then Bingham began to speak clearly, loudly, and distinctly, all the while staring at Sir Thomas, who looked alternately at the glass and the floor.

"No one would have benefitted greatly by the death of either Lord Bodley or Lady Jenny," Bingham said. "That is why, Your Honor, I submit that the poison was not intended for either person. It was Duke Tilden Withington's drink that contained the poison. It was Duke Withington who took the drink into the glade and set it on the table where it was drunk, not by the duke, but mistakenly by Lord Bodley. The poison was intended neither for Bodley, nor for Jenny, but for Duke Tilden Withington."

Sir Thomas began gulping water convulsively. Jenny gasped as did most of the other occupants of the courtroom.

"All we need to do now is discover who handed the drink to Duke Withington, and then we will know the identity of our murderer," Bingham stated simply.

"And I'm sure Duke Withington knows who handed him that drink, just as he knows who invited him to that engagement party." Bingham kept his eyes firmly on Sir Thomas, who seemed to be trying to sink into the chair. The witness licked his very dry lips and seemed to be gasping for air. He would not raise his eyes.

Bingham continued relentlessly. "It was Duke Tilden Withington who would take Lady Jennifer Greenough away and leave the Cottinghams without the financial means to which they had become accustomed. If Duke Withington took Jenny away, he would also remove the Cottinghams' entry into royal circles, for he would be taking away the money that is so much the mark of today's leisurely gentleman.

"No one would even know that Sir Thomas knew Duke Withington," Bingham continued, his voice filled with the confidence of a lawyer who knew his case was won. "So he would not be suspected. Lady Diane had been in America for sixteen years and would be informed that her daughter wanted no part of her or the inheritance. Jenny would live unhappily ever after with Lord Bodley, and the Cottinghams would live splendidly on the profits from Cottingham's sale of this beautiful, unsuspecting young lady to the infamous Lord Bodley. Was the entire family in on the deception as they were involved in the deceit the night Jenny was snatched so cruelly from her mother's arms?"

Bingham's voice had risen with that last question. For the first time in many minutes, Sir Thomas met the eyes of his accuser. Sir Thomas stood, and his eyes bulged as he looked out and pointed toward Lady Diane. "It all started with her," he accused. "I knew she was unhappy with William Greenough. I tried to console her, but no, she wouldn't confide in me. She was loyal to her husband, so I thought. But then Duke Stanford Withington changed all that. She simply preferred any man to me."

The judge ordered Sir Thomas to sit down. He staggered back into his seat and took a sip from the glass. Some of the water drooled from the side of his mouth. He didn't wipe it away.

Lady Christine buried her face in her hands. She had often accused her husband of loving Diane, but she hadn't really believed it. Everyone's eyes were fastened on Sir Thomas, and the judge did nothing to keep the man from incriminating himself.

"Jenny looked so much like Diane," Sir Thomas was saying, in a distant voice. "I really cared for that little girl. That's why I joined in on the kidnaping scheme. I didn't want Jenny taken away too. Lord Greenough had everything, but he was too demanding, too loud, too mean for a lady like Diane. I deserved her and Jenny. I could have handled the money, but he was squandering it. I kept telling him the way he was bringing Jenny up wasn't right. I talked for years. Finally he began to relent, but by that time my finances were in disastrous shape."

Sir Thomas looked about helplessly, as if appealing for sympathy. "He was about to die anyway. He was finished." The man's shoulders slumped and his voice became lower. "I did provide for Jenny. I used her money, yes. But my daughter and wife needed it. They needed those things to make them happy, to make them respect me."

Sir Thomas cleared his throat and in a trembling voice continued. "I loved Christine and Emmaline. It's just that this other thing is a weakness, shall we say. Then the younger brother of the man who took Diane away came to take Jenny away. Jenny would know that her mother was not dead. There would be questions. What else could I do? Let everyone know where my wealth came from? My friends? My wife? My daughter?"

He shrugged helplessly. "I knew what I had to do when I invited Duke Tilden Withington to the party. Then I saw him when he first looked at Jenny. I knew he was thinking she was as beautiful as her mother and would never let her marry Bodley if he could prevent it. And Jenny didn't want to marry Bodley."

Lady Diane wiped away the tears that streaked her face,

tears shed for Christine and Emmaline. She knew so well the pain of heartbreak, estrangement from a loved one, a troubled mind, and accusations. She longed to tell Thomas that the Lord could forgive him, give him a certain kind of acceptance and peace, although he would still have to pay for the terrible things he had done.

"I knew what I had to do," Thomas said, his voice suddenly bold, but his eyes glazed. Bingham stepped back, almost behind him, allowing Sir Thomas to be the center of attention.

"I poured a round of drinks," Sir Thomas said, "and as I did, at one moment I stopped and pretended to take the snuff from my snuff box, like this." He took out the silver box and demonstrated. "Then I emptied the contents into a glass, poured several drinks, and handed them out. I gave the one with arsenic to Duke Tilden Withington, placed the snuff box that had contained the arsenic back into my inside pocket, poured other drinks, and handed them out as well. No one knew or even suspected what I had done. Upon my person, I had two of the silver tins, and I disposed of the incriminating one when I left Bodley House to fetch the doctor."

Before anyone could react, Sir Thomas emptied the contents of his snuff box into the glass beside him, stirred with his finger, and gulped it down. In shocked silence, all eyes watched as he sank dejectedly into the chair. The glass clinked to the floor.

Murmurs rose through the courtroom. Emmaline screamed. Lady Christine gasped in disbelief. The judge called for the courtroom to be cleared and for a doctor to be summoned. In the midst of the confusion, with the spectators reluctant to leave, the relentless Bingham asked one final question to the man whose physical pain now matched his emotional anguish.

"Would you have allowed Lady Jenny to take the blame for the murder of Ignatius, Lord Bodley?"

Sir Thomas's pain ceased momentarily as he stared at Bingham. He sought out Jenny's distressed face. Finally comprehension of the depths to which he had sunk entered his eyes. He would have allowed the destruction of Diane's child. That realization was more painful to him than the physical agony that now racked his body. His eyes bulged with fear at some distant image within himself, then Sir Thomas leaned forward to bury his head in his arms against the wooden railing.

The dying man looked down and his eyes fastened upon the glass that had rolled along the hardwood floor in front of him. The last thing he saw was the white powdery ring around its inside edge.

fifteen

Jenny stood starboard, alone, looking at the white frothy foam made by the waves of the vast ocean. She would look back for only a moment, remembering the last few days and Uncle Thomas's funeral. It had been a great embarrassment to Aunt Christine and Emmaline, for no one had attended the event save family members. The Cottinghams were now social outcasts, as her mother had been for so many years.

But Jenny and her mother both found that with divine help they were able, not only to forgive, but also to share the source of strength they had received from God. They both realized that Thomas had suffered a gradual decline in character after having set in motion a chain of events that led to his eventual self-destruction.

"We are ruined," Aunt Christine had wailed desperately. "Oh, Diane, for the first time I realize what you must have gone through. How can we live with the ostracization and ridicule that will surely come?"

Jenny's mother had implored them to return to America with her. "It will be a new start for the two of you. I think you both will learn to love it." Emmaline looked forward to such an adventure, and Aunt Christine gratefully accepted the invitation.

Yes, Jenny thought as she stared out at the sea, *I have come through the valley of the shadow of death.* Only one shadow was upon her life now, and that was the impossible love she felt for Tilden. Her mother, aunt, and cousin were being so brave, enduring the harsh realities of life, so perhaps with time, she could learn to endure a life without Tilden.

She would not allow the past and its troubles to distract her now, but watched the great ship steer toward the setting sun, which painted the sky in streaks of red and gold. Tomorrow, the sun would rise on a new day, a new life.

Hearing footfalls she assumed were those of her mother, Jenny turned. "Mama—"

Jenny was stunned into silence. Her mother was nowhere to be seen. Instead Tilden walked toward her, causing her heart to leap like the frothy tips of the waves. The reflection of the water, gold from the last rays of the sun, gave her countenance an ethereal glow.

Tilden simply stared at her, and she mistook his silence for displeasure. She had done him a terrible injustice. "I'm so sorry that I ever suspected you of murdering Lord Bodley, or of making an attempt on my life," she said.

"I too had my doubts about you upon occasion," he confessed. "I admit to having had windmills in my head."

"You. . .you forgive me?" she asked hesitantly.

"I would forgive you anything," he replied, then added, "with one exception."

"Wh. . .what?" Suddenly she found it difficult to breathe, for her chest had tightened when he came so close to her. His wonderful face bent toward hers, and his eyes held that special glow.

"I could never forgive you, Jenny, if you didn't allow me to say what I've wanted to tell you from the moment I saw you at Bodley House." He drew in his breath. "I love you, Jenny. I want to marry you. I want to live my life with you."

Her eyes danced, and inscrutable joy graced her beautiful face. "I thought. . .you and my mother—"

"You were wrong." He grasped her hands and came even nearer. "Lady Diane and I are like older sister and younger brother. But I couldn't explain that to you when you thought I was a murderer. You would have also judged me a liar and would have had no reason to believe my words. But believe me, Jenny, I've never loved any woman the way I love you. I've never wanted another to become my wife. Oh, Jenny. There will never be another. Only you, my dearest."

Jenny closed her eyes and drew in her breath as if his words were unendurable.

Not sure what she was feeling, Tilden added, "If you think you could love me, Jenny, let me know. If not, tell me and I will go away and try not to see you, for that would be torture. But please know, I love you dearly, with all my heart."

Finally Jenny found her voice. "I love you with all my heart. And I think, Tilden," she whispered, her pink lips trembling with emotion, "that you should kiss me, lest I swoon from the want of it."

The light leaped into Tilden's face. "Oh, Jenny!" He swooped her into his arms, swung her around, then set her on her feet again and tenderly drew her near. His lips found hers, and they met in a lingering, tender kiss of love, as their hearts united and they committed themselves to each other.

Finally Tilden moved his lips away long enough to ask softly, "Where did you learn to kiss like that?"

With a beautiful upturned face and eyes shining, she murmured, "There was once, in a lovely glade, a stranger—"

Tilden's arms tightened around her and his heart raced. The brilliant red and golden glints of sun danced around them, while inside he burned with tomorrow's promise, ignited by love's eternal flame. Just before he again claimed her lips as his own, he said huskily, "Strangers no more."

A Letter To Our Readers

Dear Reader:

In order that we might better contribute to your reading enjoyment, we would appreciate your taking a few minutes to respond to the following questions. We welcome your comments and read each form and letter we receive. When completed, please return to the following:

Rebecca Germany, Fiction Editor
Heartsong Presents
PO Box 719
Uhrichsville, Ohio 44683

1. Did you enjoy reading *The Stranger's Kiss* by Yvonne Lehman?
   - ❏ Very much! I would like to see more books by this author!
   - ❏ Moderately. I would have enjoyed it more if

   _____

   _____

2. Are you a member of **Heartsong Presents**? Yes ❏ No ❏
   If no, where did you purchase this book?_____

   _____

3. How would you rate, on a scale from 1 (poor) to 5 (superior), the cover design?_____

4. On a scale from 1 (poor) to 10 (superior), please rate the following elements.

   _____ Heroine   _____ Plot

   _____ Hero   _____ Inspirational theme

   _____ Setting   _____ Secondary characters

5. These characters were special because_____

_____

_____

6. How has this book inspired your life?_____

_____

_____

7. What settings would you like to see covered in future
   Heartsong Presents books?_____

_____

_____

8. What are some inspirational themes you would like to see
   treated in future books?_____

_____

_____

9. Would you be interested in reading other **Heartsong
   Presents** titles?   Yes ❑   No ❑

10. Please check your age range:
    ❑ Under 18   ❑ 18-24   ❑ 25-34
    ❑ 35-45   ❑ 46-55   ❑ Over 55

Name _____

Occupation _____

Address _____

City _____ State _____ Zip _____

Email _____

the Sewing Circle

Edna Tidewell is a Titus woman. Following the Biblical injunction to mentor younger women in Christ, this pastor's wife sets aside each Tuesday afternoon for the young women of Hickory Corners, Ohio. During "Tea with Mrs. T," the ladies do personal sewing or hold a quilting bee while Mrs. Tidewell reads aloud from the Scriptures. Discussion, tea, and sweet conversation round out each afternoon.

These special get-togethers could have far-reaching effects on four young ladies.

Relax along the banks of the historic Ohio River and watch four searching young women transform into stable servants of the Lord. Their stories will warm your heart and inspire your soul.

paperback, 352 pages, 5 ³⁄₁₆" x 8"

♥ ♥ ♥ ♥ ♥ ♥ ♥ ♥ ❤ ♥ ♥ ♥ ♥ ♥ ♥ ♥ ♥

♥ ♥ ♥ ♥ ♥ ♥ ♥ ♥ ❤ ♥ ♥ ♥ ♥ ♥ ♥ ♥ ♥

·····Hearts♥ng·····

HISTORICAL ROMANCE IS CHEAPER BY THE DOZEN!

Any 12 *Heartsong Presents* titles for only $26.95 *

Buy any assortment of twelve *Heartsong Presents* titles and save 25% off of the already discounted price of $2.95 each!

*plus $1.00 shipping and handling per order and sales tax where applicable.

HEARTSONG PRESENTS TITLES AVAILABLE NOW:

(If ordering from this page, please remember to include it with the order form.)

·······Presents·······

Great Inspirational Romance at a Great Price!

Heartsong Presents books are inspirational romances in contemporary and historical settings, designed to give you an enjoyable, spirit-lifting reading experience. You can choose wonderfully written titles from some of today's best authors like Peggy Darty, Sally Laity, Tracie Peterson, Colleen L. Reece, Lauraine Snelling, and many others.

When ordering quantities less than twelve, above titles are $2.95 each.
Not all titles may be available at time of order.